DOLLEY'S GHOST WAS PLAYING WITH FIRE . . .

Mr. Rexon took center stage. "President Wright, Mr. Wright, ladies and gentlemen, as you know, we are here this evening to witness the official unveiling of President Wright's portrait, which will soon take its place in history among . . ."

Suddenly Molly had an overwhelming feeling of dread, the *same* feeling she had had just before the marble bust fell on Jam. Trouble was brewing, and Molly was sure Dolley was behind it.

Out of the corner of her eye, Molly caught something flickering. On the wall to one side of the platform, long heavy damask draperies hung to the floor. Suddenly a small flame raced up along one edge and licked the ceiling.

Molly's mind was racing. What could possibly be so important to Dolley that she was willing to set the White House on fire to get her attention?

Molly shivered with fear.

She knew if she didn't figure it out soon, someone would *really* get hurt next time.

Books by Gibbs Davis

WHITE HOUSE GHOSTHUNTERS
#1 Money Madness
#2 Nest Egg Nightmare
#3 Dolley's Detectives

Available from MINSTREL Books

WHITE HOUSE GHOSTHUNTERS

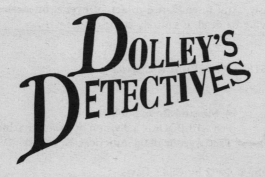

DOLLEY'S DETECTIVES

GIBBS DAVIS

A MINSTREL® BOOK

Published by POCKET BOOKS
New York London Toronto Sydney Tokyo Singapore

This book is a work of fiction. Names, characters, places and incidents are products of the author's imagination or are used fictitiously. Any resemblance to actual events or locales or persons, living or dead, is entirely coincidental.

A MINSTREL PAPERBACK *Original*

 A Minstrel Book published by
POCKET BOOKS, a division of Simon & Schuster Inc.
1230 Avenue of the Americas, New York, NY 10020

Copyright © 1997 by Gibbs Davis

All rights reserved, including the right to reproduce
this book or portions thereof in any form whatsoever.
For information address Pocket Books, 1230 Avenue
of the Americas, New York, NY 10020

ISBN: 0-671-56857-4

First Minstrel Books printing March 1997

10 9 8 7 6 5 4 3 2 1

A MINSTREL BOOK and colophon are registered trademarks of
Simon & Schuster Inc.

Cover art by Paul Blumstein

Printed in the U.S.A.

For Nancy

THE WHITE HOUSE

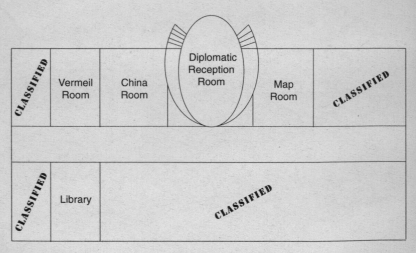

GROUND FLOOR

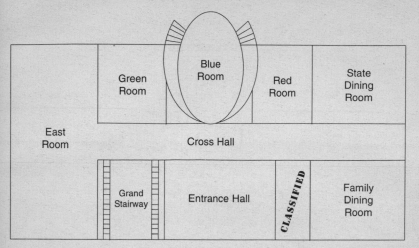

FIRST FLOOR

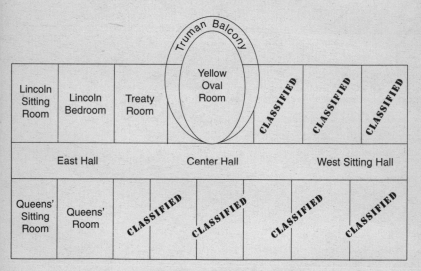

SECOND FLOOR

DOLLEY'S DETECTIVES

CHAPTER

1

"Hurry up, Jam! I'm dying to go swimming!" Twelve-year-old Molly Wright raced ahead of her younger brother toward the White House.

"Wait for me!" Jam shouted, hopping after Molly on one foot. One of his flip-flops had fallen off as he was trying to keep up with her. Boomer, his ever-present Newfoundland, quickly retrieved it and lumbered after him. The kids' Secret Service agents, Mike and Roy, hurried across the South Lawn, never losing sight of the president's children.

"I'm not waiting for anyone," Molly muttered, charging ahead. It was too blasted hot. In fact, it was the worst heatwave in Washington, D.C.'s history. And to make matters worse, the White House air conditioning was broken and their mother, President Wright, had refused to have it repaired. Molly had nearly dropped dead when she heard her mother announce to the press, "The First Family hopes to set an example for every American family by using fans to conserve energy this summer."

Back in Wisconsin I'd be cooling off in a lake right now, Molly thought, hurrying past the Rose Garden. But ever since her mother had been elected president last fall and the family had moved to Washington, D.C., nothing had been the same.

Molly spotted the Oval Office up ahead, where her mother worked. The White House swimming pool would be just beyond it. She licked her lips, thirsty for the delicious feel of cool water on her skin. The instant the swimming pool came into sight, Molly broke into a run. Just as she reached the pool's edge and was about to dive in, she glanced down.

Molly gasped in horror. She stopped so suddenly that Jam crashed right into her.

"Hey, what's going on?" Jam pushed his glasses back up on his small face and stared into the bone-dry pool. Boomer barked down at a handful of men working in the bottom.

"What happened to the water?" Molly asked.

"Had to empty it to retile the pool," one of the workmen answered. "Monsieur Pigot's orders."

"Who's he?" Molly took pride in the fact that she had memorized nearly all of the ninety-two names of the White House staff.

"Some fancy French decorator," the workman answered, putting another tile into place. Red, white, and blue tiles were taking the shape of an enormous United States flag.

Molly tried to imagine looking at the stars and stripes over and over as she swam up and down the length of the pool. The thought of it made her dizzy.

Just then the French doors to the Oval Office swung open and President Wright stepped out. "How do you like it?" she asked, joining her children by the pool.

Molly made a face. "Don't you think the flag's kind of overkill, Mom?"

"Monsieur Pigot calls it playfully patriotic."

"Who is this French Peejo guy?" Molly asked, struggling to pronounce his name.

"P-I-G-O-T, *Peezhyo,*" corrected her mother. "And he's not French. He's of French descent. Naturally I couldn't hire anyone but an American to redecorate the White House."

"He's redecorating the *whole* house?" Molly asked. The White House had one hundred and thirty-two rooms!

"Not quite," President Wright said. "Just the state-rooms and our living quarters. Any special requests for your bedrooms?"

"Yeah," Molly grumbled. "Leave mine alone."

"Can he wallpaper my room with dollar bills?" Jam piped up.

Molly rolled her eyes. "Don't you ever think about anything but money?" Jam was the only seven-year-old boy she knew who wanted to grow up to be the United States Treasurer instead of a fireman or a cowboy.

"I'm afraid decorating with U.S. currency is against the law," President Wright said. "But we could compromise and paint your room the same color green as a dollar bill."

"Yeah!" Jam's eyes seemed to light up with dollar signs.

President Wright slipped an arm around Molly's shoulders. "How about you, honey?"

"I don't want some stranger messing around in my room," she said, thinking of the secret Ghosthunter Files in her computer.

"How about a new PRIVATE—KEEP OUT sign for our resident detective?" her mother teased.

Molly sighed, exasperated. Her mother rarely seemed to take her detective work seriously. But then, neither of her parents believed in ghosts, even though they lived in the most famous *and* the most haunted house in the country. Molly had already met the ghosts of two famous dead presidents since she'd moved to the White House—Abraham Lincoln and Thomas Jefferson. But as many times as she tried to convince her parents of this, they just refused to believe.

All the talk was making Molly hotter. She couldn't wait one second longer to go swimming. "Come on, Jam. Looks like we'll just have to use the indoor pool."

President Wright stopped them. "Sorry, kids. Monsieur Pigot just had the indoor pool repainted."

Molly groaned. Who was this new decorator? He was ruining her summer.

"Besides, Molly, did you forget our appointment to spend some time together today?" President Wright held up two gardening trowels. "June is the perfect month for transplanting roses."

"Why bother growing roses when you can just order them from the White House florist shop?" Molly grumbled. But she knew her mother was as fanatic about gardening as her astronomer father was about studying the sky's mysteries.

President Wright wasn't taking "no" for an answer. She had already removed her suit jacket and was rolling up her sleeves. "Care to join us, Jam?"

"No, thanks. I'm gonna check out some more license plates." He and Boomer headed across the South Lawn, with Roy following behind them. Since the end of the school year at Woodburn Academy, Jam had taken up a new hobby, memorizing tourists' out-of-state license plates and their state mottoes.

"New Hampshire!" Molly called out, testing him.

"Live Free or Die!" Jam shouted back.

Molly shook her head. "You've got a weird kid, Mom."

"Some might say I've got *two* weird kids," President Wright said, placing a trowel in Molly's hand.

Molly looked at her mother's pale blue silk blouse and skirt. "Aren't you going to change?"

"I only have one hour before I meet with Vice President Klein," she said, slipping off her high heels and heading for the Rose Garden in her bare feet. "But that's plenty of time to transplant the roses, do a little weeding, and catch up with my only daughter." She gave Molly's hand a squeeze.

Molly made a face, but she was secretly pleased. She rarely got a chance to spend time alone with her mother since she'd been elected president.

Tony, the White House head gardener, was waiting for them in the Rose Garden. He touched the brim of his hat in a silent greeting.

President Wright pointed to a thick green hedge lining one side of the garden. "Perhaps the roses would stand out more if they were in front of the boxwood. Don't you think so, Molly?"

Molly shrugged and blew a lock of reddish-brown hair off her perspiring forehead. All she could think about was diving into a pool of cool water. And her mother's new decorator had made sure that wasn't going to happen.

President Wright turned her attention to the gardener. "As you can see, my daughter isn't in a flower-planting mood. What do you think about my idea, Tony?"

The lines in Tony's face deepened as he squinted into the sun. "Don't think it much matters where you put 'em. She's not gonna like it."

President Wright looked puzzled. "She?"

"President Madison's wife," he explained, digging a hole with his shovel. "She loved this old garden. Planted the first roses here herself back in 1810. They say someone tried to move them once before and she came back to haunt 'em."

Molly stared at the gardener as if he had just turned into the most interesting person in the world. "You mean her *ghost* came back?"

"That's what they say."

President Wright shook her head with a chuckle. "Don't encourage her, Tony. My daughter has some strange notions about ghosts in the White House. Besides, I don't think Mrs. Madison is going to be a problem. After all, President James Madison and his wife have been dead for well over a hundred years."

Tony just shook his head and kept digging.

"Come on, honey," Molly's mother said. "Get your head out of the clouds and help me weed this flower bed."

Molly knelt beside her mother on the cool grass. As she began pulling out weeds, she reflected on more exciting times. Last month she had been a bridesmaid in this same garden for her handsome piano teacher's wedding to Tatiana, the Russian minister's maid. Molly sighed, remembering how Thomas Jefferson's ghost had led her to the Russians' missing Imperial Fabergé Egg. And how thrilling it had been when she and her best friend, Ama, had encountered their first ghost in the White House, Abraham Lincoln. That's when they had decided to become professional ghosthunters with their own secret club, which they called the White House Ghosthunters.

Molly realized her mother had stopped weeding

and was watching her. "Summer's just begun and you're already bored, aren't you, sweetie?"

Molly just nodded. Sometimes her mother could read her thoughts like an open book.

"Why don't you and Ama play tourist and visit some art galleries and monuments?" she suggested. "You don't want to waste your first summer in D.C. just loafing around, do you?"

Molly swatted a bee buzzing around her head and nodded lazily. Actually loafing around sounded pretty good. But her mother was right. And she knew Ama was just as bored as she was.

Suddenly a shrill voice pierced the air. "Madam President! Oh, Madam President!"

Molly looked up to see a plump little man waving to get their attention. He tiptoed across the lawn toward them in rapid little steps.

"You're about to meet Monsieur Pigot," President Wright whispered to Molly. "Be polite."

Molly gritted her teeth. So this was the man responsible for emptying both swimming pools on the hottest day of the summer.

Monsieur Pigot pulled a colorful Chinese paper fan out of his jacket pocket, whipped it open and began fanning himself furiously. *"Bonjour*, Madam President. And may I say you are the loveliest flower in this garden?"

Molly rolled her eyes. Was this guy for real?

President Wright clipped a single rose and handed it to the delighted decorator.

8

"Pour moi?" Holding the rose to his face, he closed his eyes and inhaled. He clutched his heart and swooned, saying, "Ah, I'm in heaven."

"You have to die to go to heaven," Molly stated matter-of-factly.

Monsieur Pigot's eyes slowly opened. He stared down at Molly as if she were a bug. It was an instant and mutual dislike.

"Who is this darling girl?" he asked in a flat tone.

President Wright made the formal introductions. "Monsieur Pigot, meet my daughter, Molly."

Monsieur Pigot bowed his head slightly. *"Enchanté, mademoiselle."*

"What?" Molly asked, squinching up her face.

President Wright translated. "He's delighted to meet you."

"Why?" Molly asked, knowing she was being difficult.

Monsieur Pigot's lips pursed into a tight smile. "Charming child," he said, turning his back on her and giving the president his full attention. "Madam, there's a matter of urgent importance concerning the tassels on the Blue Room drapes. I'm afraid the ambience of the entire room could be destroyed if the wrong choice is made. Would you be so kind as to take a look?"

"I'm sorry, Monsieur. I'm much too busy today. I leave it to your good taste and judgment, as usual."

Monsieur Pigot clutched his chest again. "I'm overcome by your faith in me. I promise I will do my best not to disappoint you."

9

"Does he have a heart problem?" Molly whispered to her mother.

President Wright tried hard not to laugh.

"I am moved with emotion," Monsieur Pigot said through clenched teeth.

"Monsieur Pigot is an artist, dear," President Wright tried to explain.

The decorator glanced at his diamond-studded Cartier watch and let out a little gasp. "Ah, I'm late for my appointment with your marvelous chief usher, Mr. Dunbar. Such a cultured gentleman. He has graciously agreed to dine with me and go over some of the history of your magnificent home. I must bid you both adieu. *Au revoir.*" The decorator pivoted around and skittered back across the lawn, his long peacock blue scarf fluttering out behind him.

Molly couldn't resist a parting remark. "Nice to meet you, Mr. *Pig-o!*" she called, deliberately mispronouncing his name.

Monsieur Pigot stumbled at the sound of his name being mispronounced. He quickly composed himself and continued inside.

That night, Molly and Jam decided to sleep on the South Portico balcony in hopes of catching a breeze. But as she settled down for the night next to her brother, Molly stuck a finger in her mouth and raised it to the still, hot air. Nothing.

She stretched out on the inflatable air mattress she had hoped to use in the pool earlier and tried to imagine herself floating in the cool water. "I miss Wisconsin," she said with a sigh. "We'd be skinny-dipping in Lake Mendota on a night like this."

"Boomer misses it, too," Jam said, trying to squeeze onto the air mattress his dog was sprawled across. Boomer's immense furry tail beat against the ground in agreement. The Newfoundland lifted his huge head with a groan and licked Jam's perspiring face.

" 'While I breathe, I hope,' " Jam said, curling up around Boomer.

"Whose state motto is that?" Molly asked.

"South Carolina's," Jam mumbled, closing his eyes.

In seconds, Molly heard the faint snore of her brother sleeping. The only other sound was Boomer panting for breath, his massive sides heaving. Molly felt a small pang of jealousy as she looked at the sleeping pair. A night owl like her father, Molly knew she would be awake for hours. *Dad's probably up on the White House rooftop looking through his telescope right now*, she thought. She considered joining him, but she was too hot to move.

She rolled over and peered through the slats in the balcony railing down at the South Lawn. There was just enough moonlight to see someone walking in the Rose Garden. The person was wearing a long bathrobe. *It must be Mom*, Molly thought. *Only my workaholic mother would be out gardening at night in this heat.*

Molly was about to call down to her when she noticed the woman was much too short to be her mother. And she was wearing a fancy evening gown, not her mother's ratty old plaid bathrobe. Molly squinted in the dim light, trying to make out what appeared to be some sort of odd hat on the woman's head.

Wait a minute, Molly thought. What she saw wasn't a hat at all. It was a turban with a foot-long feather shooting straight up in the air!

Intrigued, Molly stood and leaned over the balcony railing for a closer look. A small creature was trailing behind the woman. In the moonlight Molly could make out a tail and four tiny feet. "A cat," she whispered.

Molly knew she should alert the Secret Service. It could be some crazy trespasser. She also knew Jam would never forgive her if she didn't show him first.

"Wake up," she said, nudging her brother with a foot.

"Huh?" Jam looked over at Molly, bleary-eyed.

"Come look. There's some crazy lady with a cat in the garden."

But when Molly pointed down at the Rose Garden, the woman and her cat began to fade. By the time Jam joined her at the railing, they had disappeared altogether!

"I don't see anyone," he said.

"She was here just a second ago," Molly insisted, searching the lawn. But there was no one in sight.

Molly wiped her perspiring face with the sleeve of her nightshirt. Was the heat making her delirious? she wondered. She had never seen someone that clearly before who had suddenly vanished into thin air . . .

Except . . .

A chill went through Molly as she finished her thought. *Except* when she had seen a ghost. She *knew* ghosts existed. Since she had moved into the White House, she had already encountered the ghosts of presidents Abraham Lincoln and Thomas Jefferson.

Had she just seen *another* ghost?

CHAPTER

2

"So where's this crazy lady?" Jam asked, still peering down at the lawn from the balcony.

"She's gone," Molly whispered, trying to make sense of what she had just seen. She felt sure she had seen a ghost. But what she didn't know was what this ghost wanted. Any professional ghosthunter knew that a dead person's spirit usually returned to haunt a place for a reason. Often the person had some unfinished business to take care of.

Molly's head was spinning. "It's too late to call Ama," she decided. "I'll have to wait and tell her first thing tomorrow morning."

In the meantime, Molly knew she had to get all the details of the ghost sighting down while they were still fresh in her mind. She got up to leave. "I'll be back, squirt. I need to type up a Ghost Report on my computer."

Jam's eyes opened wide. "A *ghost?*"

Molly just nodded and stepped over Boomer on her way to the door. As she was turning the doorknob, Jam asked her a question.

"Mol, do you think this one is a friendly ghost or . . . the other kind?"

A chill went up Molly's spine. She hadn't considered the question that Jam was almost afraid to ask. She took a deep breath, opened the door, and said, "I don't know, Jam. I guess we'll have to wait and see."

The next morning, Molly shut her bedroom door and contacted Ama on her computer. She couldn't risk anyone overhearing the details of her most recent ghost sighting on the telephone.

"Ghost sighting." Just whispering the words sent a thrill through Molly. She chuckled as she typed her message up on the computer screen, imagining Ama's reaction when she woke up to the incredible news.

Ama,
    Sorry it's so early but I couldn't wait. Last night I think I saw a ghost in the Rose Garden!

Ama didn't waste a second with her answer.

Wow! I'm jealous. You *always* get to see them first. Who do you think he was?

Molly's fingers flew across the keyboard.

You mean SHE. It was a woman, and she had a *ghost cat!* She was wearing a long old-fashioned gown and a weird turban with a feather on top. How soon can you come over?

Ama's excitement seemed to match Molly's.

How soon can you eat breakfast?
  The weather report predicts another scorcher today. Should I bring my swimsuit?

Molly's spirits dampened as she was reminded of Monsieur Pigot and the empty swimming pools.

Don't bother. I'll explain when you get here.

Molly signed off with their secret code for Ghosthunters: GH.
  "Come on, Ozzie," Molly sang to her pet parrot. "Rise and shine. The early bird gets the worm." Molly lifted the sleepy-eyed, foot-long gray bird off her perch and whisked her into the bathroom, setting her onto the curtain rod for their morning shower together. After showering, she quickly slipped on shorts and an FBI T-shirt, returned Ozzie to her perch, and hurried into the Family Dining Room.
  She found her father sipping coffee and poring over a dozen books spread over the table. With the

summer off from teaching astronomy, Mr. Wright spent most of his time trying to figure out his role as first husband.

Molly gave her father a quick peck on the cheek and sat down next to him. "Any luck, Dad?"

Mr. Wright looked up from a book titled *First Ladies, Past and Present*. "Mr. Dunbar suggested I read up on famous former first ladies. From what I can tell so far, they all seemed to give a lot of parties, so I've decided to do the same. My first social event will be the unveiling of your mother's presidential portrait."

"Sounds great," Molly said encouragingly.

Mr. Wright didn't look so sure. "I just don't want to let your mother down, Mol. She works so hard. And after all, I am the first 'first husband,' you know."

"I know, Dad. You'll do fine."

Mr. Wright nodded toward Jam's half-eaten bowl of soggy cereal and President Wright's coffee cup with her telltale pink lipstick mark. "You just missed your mother by ten minutes. Jam and Boomer already escorted her to the Oval Office. You and I are the family stragglers, as usual."

"Eggs, Miss?" A butler stepped forward to offer Molly a silver tray filled with eggs, toast, and bacon.

Molly nibbled thoughtfully on a piece of toast as she watched her father work on his party notes. Perhaps he had seen the woman in the garden, too. She *had* to ask. "Dad, did you see anything unusual through your telescope last night?"

Mr. Wright marked his place on the page and looked up at her. "Funny you should ask. As a matter of fact, yes, I did see something unusual. *Very* unusual."

Molly's eyes opened wide. Could it be that finally one of her skeptical parents had seen a ghost in the White House, too? "What was it?" she asked, leaning forward. She held her breath, not wanting to miss one syllable of his answer.

Mr. Wright stared into space as if he were reliving the moment. "If my eyes didn't deceive me, I believe I saw a comet in the constellation Hydra. Do you realize that hasn't occurred since 1664?"

Molly sank back in her chair. "That's nice, Dad," she said, deflated.

An officious reed-thin woman appeared in the doorway just then, clutching a bulging appointment book.

"Ah, Ms. Brown!" Mr. Wright said, announcing his social secretary's arrival. "I'm drowning in party details and you've come to rescue me."

Ms. Brown picked up one of the books on the table. She couldn't hide her amusement as she read the title out loud: *"Famous First Ladies in History.* Very enterprising, Mr. Wright. Did I mention that marvelous decorator, Monsieur Pigot, has offered to help with the table settings and flower arrangements? He has such a flair for entertaining."

"Monsieur Pigot?" Molly made a face that left no doubt as to her feelings. "He's ridiculous."

"There's nothing ridiculous about this Chanel

suit," Ms. Brown said, twirling around to display her new outfit. "He brought me this from his last trip to Paris." She glanced at her watch and stopped mid-twirl, suddenly all business. "Time to go over the menu, Mr. Wright. We're late for our appointment with the head chef."

"Yes, yes, of course," Mr. Wright said, fumbling with his notes. On the way out he planted a quick kiss on Molly's head and handed her an envelope with the presidential seal. "I almost forgot. Your mother asked me to give you this."

As soon as Molly was alone, she opened it. Inside was an official-looking letter in her mother's hand-writing on White House stationery. With her busy schedule, President Wright often resorted to leaving notes in her children's backpacks or on their pillows at bedtime.

Dear Molly,

Sorry to miss you.

Monsieur Pigot informs me this morning he found all the furniture and paintings he moved yesterday returned to their original places. He seems to suspect that you are responsible.

Darling, I realize it's been a difficult summer and you're bored, but please try to cooperate. Monsieur Pigot has been very helpful to your father and me.

Hugs and Kisses,
Mom

P.S. I haven't heard any piano scales lately. Don't forget to practice.

Molly's cheeks burned with anger as she reread the decorator's accusation. "I can't believe it," she said, crumpling the letter into a tight ball. "That creep is making up lies to get me in trouble."

Just then a butler appeared in the doorway with an announcement. "Miss Wright, Ama Afriyie has just arrived. She's waiting for you in the Rose Garden."

"Thanks, Alphonso," Molly said, heading for the First Family's private elevator. She knew her friend couldn't wait to investigate the place where the ghost had been sighted the night before.

"Perfect timing," Molly whispered as she pushed the elevator button for the ground floor.

There was just one problem. She couldn't decide which she wanted to do more—hunt for a ghost or kill a decorator.

After questioning the gardening staff and checking the Rose Garden for any evidence of ghosts, Molly and Ama decided to cool off in the White House's cavernous East Room. The huge room, reserved for White House dances and entertainment, was a natural roller-skating rink.

"Pig-o is decorating in the East Room today," Molly explained, sitting on the hall floor to strap on her rollerblades. "This'll drive him crazy."

Ama's long brown legs wobbled on her roller-blades as she gazed down at Molly, unconvinced. "Come on, Mol. How bad can one little decorator be?"

"You'll see." Molly motioned for Ama to follow as she skated down the length of the long Cross Hall onto the East Room's gleaming oak floors.

They found Monsieur Pigot and Mr. Dunbar standing by a window comparing curtain fabrics. The decorator had turned Mr. Dunbar into a makeshift curtain rod, draping several lengths of fabric over the stretched-out arms of the diminutive chief usher. As soon as they spotted the girls, the two men started talking to each other in French.

"Heads up!" Molly shouted, skating straight for them at top speed. She sailed between the startled men, grabbing hold of one of the rolls of cloth. It sailed out behind her, unwinding across the floor in one long rippled wave of color.

Monsieur Pigot clutched his heart and muttered something to Mr. Dunbar in French. Mr. Dunbar nodded in agreement.

Monsieur Pigot waved them away. "I'm sorry, children, but you'll have to leave *tout de suite*. Mr. Dunbar and I are consulting on the East Room today, and we simply cannot be disturbed."

Molly rolled to a stop by the piano and plopped down on the bench. She glared at Monsieur Pigot, her fingers poised over the keyboard. "My mother wants me to practice the piano. Should I tell the president you object?''

The decorator's smug expression withered as he backed away. "By all means, practice your divine instrument. Music is my inspiration."

"I call this piece *Chinese Water Torture*,'' Molly whispered to Ama with a devilish grin. She struck a single key and began playing the same scale over and over, painstakingly slowly.

In minutes, the frazzled decorator had his hands pressed against his ears. "I surrender!" he cried in French. "I can't work with these little monsters!"

"I agree," Mr. Dunbar answered in French.

"Watch this," Ama whispered to Molly. She skated up to the two men and spoke to them with an impeccable French accent.

Monsieur Pigot's mouth dropped open as Ama laughed at their amazed reaction. He fled the room with Mr. Dunbar chasing after him, but the decorator was inconsolable.

A moment later Mr. Dunbar marched back into the East Room and glared down at Molly through his thick glasses. "You know, Miss Wright, you could learn something about style and grace from Monsieur Pigot," he said, eyeing her T-shirt and shorts. "He studied at a top fashion house in Europe. I can't tell you what a pleasure it is to finally have a man of refinement and taste working on our staff, and I intend to make him feel welcome." He spun around on his heels and exited the room.

Molly was more interested in knowing what Ama had said to ruffle Monsieur Pigot's feathers. She often marveled at her friend's many hidden accomplishments. "I didn't know you could speak French," she said to Ama.

"I speak several languages," Ama remarked casually as she skated a circle eight around the piano. "My native language in Ghana was Akan, but we all spoke French in school."

"Well?"' Molly was bursting to know. "What did you say?"

"Monsieur Pigot said we were little monsters, and I said there are no monsters in France, only bad decorators."

Molly laughed out loud. "I told you Pigot was a creep. Anyway, he'll think twice before he spreads any more lies about me moving his furniture around again."

Ama nodded and skated toward the door. "I'd better get going. I promised to babysit Kena this afternoon." She had a little brother the same age as Jam.

After Ama left, Molly decided to take her mother's advice and practice the piano, after all. Besides, the East Room was one of the coolest rooms in the house.

Sitting on the piano bench, she decided to play one of the first compositions she had ever learned. She closed her eyes and began playing it by heart. All the frustrations of the past few days melted away as she listened to her music fill the room.

Suddenly an icy-cold breeze swept over her.

Molly's fingers froze in place. She had the eerie sensation of someone nearby watching her. Her eyes flew open. What she saw made her gasp with fright.

Directly in front of her, only inches away, a heavy porcelain vase hovered in midair!

CHAPTER

3

Before Molly had a chance to blink, the vase floated across the room and dropped to the floor with a loud crash.

Molly leaped up from the piano bench, her eyes darting around the room, searching for the culprit. But she was alone. Her heart raced as she put together the incredible facts. A sudden drop in temperature, the strong feeling of another human presence, and, most incredible of all, a vase flying through the air on its own. *It could only add up to one thing*, Molly thought.

"A ghost," she whispered, goosebumps dotting her arms.

Realizing that as a professional ghosthunter, she should immediately examine the evidence, Molly wished Ama were still there so she wouldn't have to do it alone.

"Just pretend you're Nancy," she whispered to herself. Whenever Molly was scared, she conjured up the image of the daring heroine in the Nancy Drew mysteries to help push her through her fear.

Molly took a deep breath and slowly skated toward the shattered vase. She knelt on one knee and carefully picked up one of the broken pieces. There were no strings attached. Clearly, this was the work of a mischievous spirit. She turned it over in her hand, hoping to find a clue.

Just then her mother entered the room, followed by a small entourage of secretaries and advisors. "I thought I heard piano music. You sounded lovely," President Wright said as she walked up to Molly, stooped over the broken vase. "What's this?" she asked, taking the jagged piece of porcelain from Molly's hand. "Have you been rollerblading in here again?"

Molly nodded, her cheeks burning with embarrassment. She knew it looked bad. "I didn't break it though," she tried to explain, the words tumbling out nonstop. "It fell. I mean, it flew across the room and then it fell. I'm almost sure a ghost did it. Really, Mom. First the room got really cold and then—"

President Wright held up a hand to stop her. "Molly, it's one thing to have an active imagination and quite another to make up wild excuses. We all have to take responsibility for our actions."

"But, Mom—"

"I'm sure it was an accident, honey. But you have to remember the White House doesn't belong to us. We're just temporary residents living here for my term of office, and this eighteenth-century vase was a piece of priceless American history."

Molly yanked off her rollerblades. "Fine. Don't believe me," she said, stomping out of the room in her socks.

On her way out she overheard her mother say to her staff, "I'm sure it's the heat. She's just a little cranky."

Molly spent the rest of the afternoon cooling off in her bedroom. She took a cold shower and turned on all of her three fans. She had to think clearly. Something strange was going on, and Molly was determined to get to the bottom of it.

"Time to do a little ghost research," she said, setting her parrot down on top of her computer monitor. "I don't get it, Ozzie. All the other White House ghosts were helpful. But this one breaks stuff and gets me in trouble."

She sat down at her computer desk and switched on the power. "Prepare for takeoff, Commander Ozzie," she said, listening to the familiar hum of the computer starting up.

"Fasten your seat belts! Fasten your seat belts!" Ozzie squawked, flapping her long gray wings. The parrot dropped her small head upside down over the edge of the computer monitor and waited for something to come up on the screen.

Molly logged on to the Internet, ran the Web Browser and typed in *www.loc.gov.*, the Web address of the Library of Congress. In no time, an image of the world's largest library appeared on her screen, and she began pulling up information on different types of ghosts.

She scanned the screen, looking for the description that would fit her troublemaking ghost:

Ghost Type 1—Ghosts of the dead who are seen repeatedly.
Ghost Type 2—Ghosts of the dead who are seen once or twice.
Ghost Type 3—Ghost of a dying person.
Ghost Type 4—Ghosts of the dead who talk.
Ghost Type 5—Ghosts of living people.
Ghost Type 6—Poltergeists.

"Poltergeists," Molly said, highlighting the strange new word. She quickly read through the description on her screen.

Poltergeists are noisy spirits who haunt specific people, rather than places. They are usually found indoors and almost always cause trouble.

Poltergeists often move objects, sometimes breaking them. Their mischief can be harmful. Some poltergeists have been known to bite people or throw heavy pieces of furniture.

If you have encountered a poltergeist, beware.

They are the most dangerous type of ghost.

"This is it," Molly whispered. "But what would a poltergeist want from me?"

Suddenly the computer screen flickered and died.

The following morning, Molly woke from a fitful sleep, her legs twisted in her sheets. She had dreamed an invisible poltergeist was hurling vases at her, one after another.

Molly checked the barometer outside her bedroom window. It was a stifling ninety-one degrees and climbing. She immediately called Ama, and they arranged to meet in an air-conditioned shopping mall in nearby Georgetown.

When she met up with Ama at a department store at the mall, Molly was dying to tell her about the poltergeist. But her Secret Service agent, Mike, was never more than a few feet behind them, wearing his trademark sunglasses and dark blue suit.

"Follow me," Molly whispered to Ama. She grabbed some clothes off a boutique rack and ducked into the nearest dressing room. Part of learning the ropes as first daughter included finding privacy whenever she could. Molly had quickly learned that bathrooms and dressing rooms were off-limits, even to Secret Service agents.

As soon as the girls were out of earshot, Molly filled in her friend on the flying-vase incident. "It's definitely the work of a poltergeist," she said, trying on a big floppy hat that covered half her face. It would be a perfect disguise for future outings.

Ama didn't look convinced. "Maybe . . . or maybe that decorator is just playing tricks on you."

Molly stared at her self-assured friend as Ama modeled a sundress. She hadn't considered that possibility. It was fun having a ghosthunting partner, but sometimes Molly wished Ama wasn't so good at figuring out all the angles. It made things more complicated, and besides, sometimes Molly just wanted to be right.

Later that afternoon, when Molly returned to the White House, she was greeted by a stampede of feet thundering down the grand stairway. "Watch out!" Jam shouted, racing down the stairs after Boomer.

The huge dog barreled into Molly, nearly knocking her off her feet, and continued running out of the Entrance Hall. The only time she could remember seeing Boomer move that fast was when he chased squirrels outside.

"Hey, what's going on?" Molly shouted after her brother.

Jam ran past Molly in hot pursuit of the frantic Newfoundland. "Dunno! Boomer's after something!"

"Weird kid." Molly picked up her shopping bags

and slowly climbed the stairs to the private family rooms on the second floor.

For the first time in days, Monsieur Pigot was nowhere to be seen. *What a relief,* Molly thought. It would be the perfect time to take a cold shower and finish her Ghost Report on the flying-vase incident.

At the top of the stairs, Molly heard a door close and looked up the long hallway. A butler was leaving her room. He flipped a scarf over his shoulder and started up the hall.

Molly instantly recognized the rapid little steps. It wasn't a butler at all. It was Monsieur Pigot! Her cheeks burned with anger as she blocked his path. "What were you doing in my room?" she demanded.

"Simply trying to save it from bad taste, dear." He breezed past her and disappeared down the stairs.

Molly was fuming. This was the last straw. No one was allowed to enter her private sanctuary without her permission. Not even Mrs. Thompkins, the head maid, cleaned without Molly being present. All of her secret Ghost Files and notebooks were hidden in her bedroom. "He's not getting away with this," Molly vowed. "I'm telling Mom."

But first Molly had to see what Monsieur Pigot had done. She flew down the hall and burst into her room.

Molly uttered a gasp of disbelief. Her bedroom was unrecognizable. All her furniture had been rearranged and swatches of fabric were draped over every surface. Even Ozzie's perch had a blue paint chip taped to it.

"Abandon ship! Abandon ship!" Ozzie squawked, flapping her wings.

Molly raced over to her computer. Ama would know what to do. "I hope this thing is working now," she muttered, flipping on the power switch. But as she sat down to type her message, she landed hard on the floor.

Monsieur Pigot had taken her computer chair!

"I have to see my Mom right now. It's an emergency," Molly said, whisking past Mr. Peale, the president's secretary.

"She's in a meeting with the vice president," Mr. Peale protested.

Molly didn't care. She was tired of her needs coming last all the time, after the country's needs and now even after a nosy decorator. Enough was enough!

Molly burst into the Oval Office. "I need to talk to you!" she announced.

Startled, President Wright looked up at Molly from behind a large mahogany desk. "Molly, I'm in a meeting with Vice President Klein. Can't this wait?"

"No." Molly crossed her arms over her chest and stood her ground. She wasn't budging until she was heard.

The vice president rose from his chair. "Why don't

I give the two of you a few minutes alone together," he offered graciously.

President Wright nodded appreciatively. "Thanks, Rob."

As soon as the vice president left the room, Molly started talking nonstop. "You won't believe what happened, Mom. I caught that creepy decorator leaving my room. He rearranged everything and left his stupid fabrics and paint chips all over the place. He probably went through all my stuff. And he's a thief! He stole my old computer chair, the one I brought all the way from Wisconsin!" Tears started welling up in Molly's eyes.

"Calm down, honey." President Wright got up from her desk and put her arms around Molly. "Why do you let yourself get so upset over a little decorating? He was just doing his job."

"He went into my room without asking." Molly knew she sounded babyish, but she couldn't help it.

"Molly, you've made no secret of how you feel about Monsieur Pigot. But now you're starting to sound like the little boy who cried wolf. Everyone else has found him very helpful and friendly." President Wright led her toward the door. "We'll talk more about this later, okay? In the meantime, why don't you think about working *with* Monsieur Pigot instead of fighting him. I know he could use some help keeping track of all the changes he's making. You're good at details. It might be fun."

"Where's my computer chair?" Molly grumbled.

President Wright hesitated before answering. "Monsieur Pigot felt it was a bit . . . well, tacky, so he got rid of it. But it'll be replaced with something much nicer," she quickly added.

Before Molly had a chance to respond, her mother planted a kiss on her forehead and gave her a gentle push out the door. She motioned for the vice president to come back into the Oval Office.

"Are you two through?" Vice President Klein asked.

Molly wanted to say "no," but she realized Monsieur Pigot had already snowed her mother and all the other adults in the White House. It was clear she was on her own.

"This is war," Molly declared, marching through the long white-pillared colonnade connecting the West Wing to the Executive Residence. Her mother had given her a brainstorm. Maybe she *would* help Monsieur Pigot. Molly picked up her pace as the idea slowly formed in her mind. She would do as her mother suggested. From now on, she would take inventory of every chair, painting, and vase Monsieur Pigot moved. She would tag after him everywhere, never leaving him alone for one second. They would be inseparable.

Molly headed straight for her bedroom. She was already mentally preparing to catalog the household inventory on her computer. "I'll catalog it room by room, according to furniture and art work," she decided, sitting down at her desk. Just as her hand reached for the power switch to boot up the computer, the screen lit up by itself.

Molly's eyes froze on the message flashing on and off on the computer screen.

If you have encountered a poltergeist, beware. They are the most dangerous type of ghost.

CHAPTER

"Were those silver candlesticks you just moved from the eighteenth or nineteenth century?" Molly asked, ready to jot down Monsieur Pigot's answer in her notebook. She followed on his heels into the Blue Room.

Monsieur Pigot stopped abruptly, and Molly bumped into him. The annoyed decorator spun around, a look of rage on his face. For a second, Molly thought he might strike her.

"For the hundredth time, would you please stop following me so closely. I can hear you breathing!"

Molly smiled sweetly. "I'm just trying to be helpful."

"Dear Miss Wright," he said through clenched teeth, "wouldn't you be happier playing with your little brother?"

"Okay." Molly flipped her notebook shut and

started to walk away. "I'll tell Mom you don't want me around anymore."

"No, no, no, no!" Monsieur Pigot ran after her, fluttering his hands in protest. He led her back into the Blue Room. "We don't want to bother the president. I'm sure we can work something out. And now if you'll excuse me, I must use *la salle de bains.*"

Molly knew that was French for "the bathroom." "No problem," she chirped, following after him. She stood guard outside the bathroom door until he came out.

"Oh, you're still here. How comforting," he said, walking past her to the elevator. "Thank you for your invaluable help today. But now I must bid you adieu and spend some time alone in my studio."

Molly squeezed through the elevator doors just before they closed. "Your studio? Isn't that the storage room you keep locked all the time?"

Before Molly could get her answer, the elevator doors opened onto the third floor and they found Mr. Dunbar on the other side, giving instructions to a young maid. Mr. Dunbar's face lit up as he saw the decorator. *"Bonjour, monsieur!"*

Molly rolled her eyes as the two men embraced as though they hadn't seen each other in years, instead of since yesterday.

"May I say you're looking *trés chic,*" Monsieur Pigot commented.

Mr. Dunbar seemed to burst with pleasure as he

gave each of his jacket sleeves a tug. "You were so right about the European cut. It is superior."

Monsieur Pigot put a conspiratorial arm around the chief usher and led him away. Molly followed close behind, but it was no use trying to hear what they were saying because they were conversing in French. *If only Ama were here to translate,* she thought. Nothing annoyed her more than being kept out of a secret conversation.

Just then Boomer came racing around the corner, barking like crazy. Molly stepped back to make way for the torpedo-sized dog as he took off down the hall. She watched, incredulous, as he ran *head-first* straight into a wall! With a loud thunk, he hit the wall and then landed in a heap on the floor.

Molly hurried to the dog's side. "What's wrong, boy? What are you chasing all the time?"

Boomer lifted his head and gazed at her intently, as if trying to explain. Then he dropped his aching head into her lap with a whimper.

Molly looked up the hall for signs of Monsieur Pigot and Mr. Dunbar, but they were gone.

Molly tried to comfort Boomer as questions raced through her mind. Frightening questions.

Where did that weird noise come from? It sounded like someone snorting back a laugh. Was it Boomer?

Was Monsieur Pigot playing tricks on her, as Ama had suggested?

Or was it Mr. Dunbar?

Maybe they had teamed up to scare her?

A shiver of fear ran down her back as she heard the strange sound again—a definite giggle. She could have sworn it sounded like a *woman's* voice.

The following week, President Wright left notes for Molly every morning with the same message—which was why Molly groaned when she rolled over in bed and found yet another envelope with the presidential seal lying on her pillow on Friday.

"Here we go again," she said, reading the note aloud to her sleepy-eyed parrot.

Dear Molly,

This game you are playing on Monsieur Pigot has got to stop. After you undo all of his work every night, he is forced to start all over again the next day.

I've tried to be as fair as I can, but when all you can say is "Pig-o did it," you leave me no choice.

You have one more chance or you're grounded. It's up to you, honey.

Love, Mom

Molly was losing heart. She knew she needed to find proof the decorator was responsible for this nightly game of musical chairs.

"I'm going downstairs to give Monsieur *Pig-o* a piece of my mind," Molly announced to Ozzie as she began getting dressed. She knew the decorator was concentrating on the elegant first floor Red Room this week.

Molly took the elevator downstairs and stomped into the Red Room, ready to speak her mind. But what she saw left her speechless. Molly's eyes widened in disbelief as she stared at the walls.

The Red Room had turned *yellow!*

In fact, *everything* was yellow—the furniture, the draperies, the rug, everything!

Slowly, what had happened dawned on Molly. "Monsieur Pigot must have done this," she whispered. The edges of her mouth curled into a faint smile. "Wait'll Mom finds out. She'll kill him."

President Wright's blameless decorator had finally slipped up. He had destroyed the famous Red Room. Molly's mother would *have* to believe her now.

Fortunately Molly found her mother in the Blue Room next door, being interviewed by the editor of a national woman's magazine. Molly waved frantically from the doorway to get her mother's attention.

"Excuse me," President Wright said, getting up. "My daughter seems to need me. I'll be right back."

"That must be Molly," the editor said. "Madam President, may I ask her a few questions for the article?" The magazine's photographer raised his camera to take a photo of Molly, but President Wright blocked the lens with her hand.

"Absolutely not," President Wright said. "I am in

40

public office, *not* my family. Their lives are private."
She walked briskly into the Cross Hall to meet Molly.
"What is it? What's so urgent it couldn't wait until
after my interview?"

"That crazy decorator painted the Red Room yellow! Come see!" Molly could barely contain her excitement as she took her mother by the hand and
pulled her into the Red Room. She stared at her
mother's face, waiting for her reaction. But instead
of a look of astonishment, Mrs. Wright frowned at
Molly.

"Is this supposed to be a joke, young lady? Because
I don't think it's very funny." The president waited
for an answer with her hands on her hips.

Molly turned to look at the walls. She gasped in
horror. The yellow walls and draperies had disappeared. In a few seconds, the Red Room had mysteriously returned to its original color. Molly blinked
hard and shook her head, as if that might make
everything change back to yellow again. But it was
the same red it had always been. She looked help-
lessly at her mother. Was she going nuts?

"It was all yellow just a second ago," she whispered, blinking back tears. "Everything was yellow.
Really, Mom, I promise."

President Wright's face softened with concern as
she pressed her palm against Molly's forehead. "You
don't feel feverish. It must be the paint fumes. Inhal-
ing all this wet paint has made you delirious." She
put an arm around Molly and led her out of the

4 1

room. "I want you to get some fresh air, honey. Why don't you and Jam take Boomer out on the South Lawn for a walk?"

Molly gave a weak nod. There was no use in trying to explain the truth to her mother. Deep down in her bones, Molly knew what she had seen was real. There was no doubt this time. It wasn't Monsieur Pigot playing tricks on her.

A wave of cold fear swept over Molly.

This could only be the work of a poltergeist.

CHAPTER

Molly stuffed her tape recorder on top of the disguises in her ghosthunter backpack and headed downstairs. She found Jam in the Diplomatic Reception Room inside the private south entrance. Earlier they had planned to meet there.

Molly shifted her bulging backpack and whispered to him, "I remembered my part. Did you bring the Monopoly game?"

Jam nodded toward Boomer. The board game was strapped to the Newfoundland's broad back. "A walking table and Monopoly game in one," Jam said.

"Good dog," Molly said, patting Boomer's head. He wagged his tail, happy to be included.

"Some of the plastic houses are missing from the game," Jam said. "Maybe Boomer ate 'em and that's why he's been acting so weird lately."

Molly shook her head. "It's the paint fumes. He

just needs some fresh air," she said, mimicking her mother.

"Nice day for a picnic," Mike said, looking at Molly's backpack. Roy had already put on his sunglasses, ready to follow them outside at a moment's notice.

Molly nodded back at them with an innocent smile. She whispered in Jam's ear, "Proceed as planned." They headed across the expansive South Lawn with the Washington Monument looming in the distance. When they reached the tree-covered Children's Garden, Molly turned to Mike and Roy, following a few feet behind. "We're going to have our picnic and play Monopoly through there," she said. Pushing back some bushes and pointing to a small secluded clearing, she asked politely, "Can you give us a little privacy?"

Roy checked out the clearing and stood back, satisfied. "No problem. You kids enjoy yourselves."

Mike, who was a bachelor and had no children of his own, was less understanding. "Just don't sneak off the grounds," he warned. He still hadn't forgiven them for the night they snuck off the White House grounds and were nearly killed by some counterfeiters in the cave under the Lincoln Memorial.

"Oh, we won't go anywhere," Molly answered, adding under her breath, "not out of the city, anyway."

Mike was already alerting security headquarters of their location on his walkie-talkie wristwatch. "Nightingale and Rover picnicking in Children's Garden. Over and out."

44

Molly and Jam exchanged a grin. They were probably the only kids in the country with their own secret code names.

"See ya later, guys." Molly ducked behind the bushes with Jam and Boomer. They silently emptied the backpack and changed into their disguises. Molly wore a long blond wig and a floppy hat. Jam wore a curly black wig, an I LOVE D.C. baseball cap, and Mickey Mouse sunglasses.

"And now for the foolproof secret weapon," Molly whispered, pulling out her tape recorder. She pressed PLAY and nearly burst into giggles when she heard the sound of her own voice. It was an hour-and-a-half tape recording of her and Jam talking during one of their marathon Monopoly games. They had made it last week. As long as Mike and Roy heard them talking, the Secret Service agents wouldn't feel the need to look in on them.

Molly checked her Nancy Drew wristwatch. It was 1:35. "The tape ends at exactly 3:05," she said in a hushed voice. "We're going to have to hustle to make it all the way to the Potomac River. Ready, shrimp?"

Jam nodded, his wig shifting halfway down his forehead.

Molly led the way through the bushes to the eight-foot-high iron fence surrounding the White House grounds. They lay low until a couple of tourists walked past. Then Jam slipped through the narrow iron slats. Boomer squeezed through after him. Molly made it through last, sucking in her stomach, with Jam pulling.

"Ah, freedom," Molly said as a group of Japanese tourists walked by without recognizing them. It felt good not being stared at by strangers. It felt *normal.*

" 'Mountaineers are always free,' " Jam piped up, quoting another state motto.

"Colorado?" Molly guessed.

"Nope. West Virginia!" he shouted, catching up to his sister. She led him through the streets of Washington, D.C., stopping to refer to a map every now and then.

By the time they reached the wide, winding Potomac River, their shirts were soaked with sweat. Molly raced down a steep riverbank and collapsed on the grass. Her mouth felt like cotton. She had remembered everything but the sodas.

Jam sank down beside her. He stared dreamily at the sun sparkling on the water's surface. "Remember back in Wisconsin when it was hot like this and we'd go skinny-dipping?"

Molly nodded, too hot and tired to say "yes." She yanked off her wig and felt a slight breeze blowing in off the river cool her neck. The water looked so inviting.

Molly felt something wet land on her arm. A long string of drool had dropped from Boomer's mouth onto her bare skin. "Yuck!" She wiped it off and gave the startled dog a shove.

Boomer struggled to his feet and waded out into

the river. Suddenly a fish jumped up directly in front of him. Barking wildly, Boomer lunged into the water after it.

Molly watched the swimming dog with envy. "You know, Mr. Dunbar told me about a couple of presidents who used to go skinny-dipping in the Potomac every day."

Jam sat up. "Really?"

They looked at each other, sharing the same thought.

"I will if you will," Molly said.

After a quick check to make sure the coast was clear, they both started pulling off sneakers, shorts, and shirts.

"Last one in is a Republican!" Molly screamed, running into the water in her underwear.

"No fair! You got a head start!" Jam plowed through the water behind her.

Molly and Jam splashed each other while Boomer barked at them and dogpaddled around in circles. For the first time since she had moved into the White House, Molly felt like a normal kid again. No Secret Service agents, no strangers gaping at her, no servants around. Molly floated on her back and let the cool river water wash over her. Just as she was wishing the moment could last forever, Jam swam over to her, rocking the water.

"Hey, Mol! Who's that?" Jam pointed toward the riverbank.

Molly lifted her head to see. A woman was standing on the shore, taking rapid-fire photos of them with a zoom-lens camera.

"Stop it!" Molly demanded. "Who are you?"

The woman lowered her camera. "I'm a reporter with the *Washington Star*. I'd like to interview you two. Just a few words on how the president's kids are spending their first summer in the White House."

Jam crouched down in the water next to Molly. "She must have followed us here," he whispered, sounding scared. "What do we do?"

Molly was torn. Part of her loved the idea of seeing her photo on the front page of the newspaper. At the same time, she knew granting an interview would get her grounded for life. Their mother was a stickler for keeping her family out of the public eye.

"Sorry, but we can't!" Molly shouted back to shore. "Our mom doesn't allow us to do interviews!"

The reporter simply smiled and held up their clothes. "No interview, no clothes. So, is it a deal?"

Molly hugged herself in the water, thinking it over.

"What do we d-d-d-do?" Jam asked, shivering from the cold water.

Molly sighed. "We have no choice. We need our clothes to get home."

After Molly and Jam answered a few questions, the reporter returned their clothes. They made it back to the White House grounds by 3:03, with just two minutes to spare.

Mike and Roy were speechless as they watched the

dripping-wet children emerge from behind the bushes. Boomer bounded out after them, shaking his wet fur onto the stunned Secret Service agents.

When Mike opened his mouth to speak, Roy stopped him. "Don't ask," he warned. "Trust me. We don't want to know."

Without another word, they all walked back to the White House. When they were inside, Molly pushed Jam and Boomer into the First Family's private elevator. "Hurry. We can't let Mom see us like this. She'll know we went AWOL again." Molly sighed with relief when they reached the second floor. "We made it," she said as the doors slid open.

She burst out of the elevator straight into one of the household staff. He was doubled over, sneezing. "Ah-ah-ah-CHOO!"

When he finally straightened up and removed his handkerchief, Molly found herself face to face with Monsieur Pigot. Shaking with rage, he pointed an accusing finger at her. "You *knew* I was allergic to goldenrod, didn't you? You're the one responsible for replacing my lovely silk flower arrangements with all this!" He gestured up the hall. Vases bursting with the pollen-rich weed crowded every tabletop.

The poltergeist, Molly thought. What was she going to do? That ghost was getting her into trouble again.

Monsieur Pigot pointed to the floor and gasped. "You've dripped water all over my newly-refinished floors! They're ruined! Ah-ah-ah-CHOO!" He bent over in a sneezing fit.

"Come on, Jam." Molly grabbed her brother by the hand and ran up the hall with Boomer behind them. They had to get out of their wet clothes before their mother saw them.

Just before Molly shut her bedroom door, she heard Monsieur Pigot yell after them, "You're not going to get away with this!"

Molly leaned back against her bedroom door and closed her eyes. "Safe," she said with a sigh of relief.

Her mind was spinning. The goldenrod must have been another one of the poltergeist's games. Molly was sick of being blamed for the ghost's mischief. She *had* to get rid of her. But how?

Too tired to think, Molly decided to sleep on it. A nap would restore her deductive powers. She peeled off her damp clothes and headed for bed.

Just as she was about to climb in, she saw something move. . . . Something with a tail.

Molly froze as she stared into the round green eyes of a cat. The *same* cat she had seen that night in the Rose Garden. Only this time it was curled up on her pillow!

Molly gasped, stumbling back a few steps. In the blink of an eye, the cat vanished into thin air. Molly shook her head and blinked again. But the cat didn't reappear.

What's going on? Molly wondered. Was she so tired she was seeing things again? Were phantom cats really appearing and disappearing? Were red rooms really turning into yellow rooms and then back again to red?

At closer look, Molly noticed a small round indentation on the pillow. She touched it. The ghost cat had left a very *real* warm spot!

"Get a hold of yourself," Molly scolded herself. She punched the pillow and forced herself to stretch out on her bed. "The heat's just getting to me, that's all. Nancy Drew wouldn't let herself go nuts over something like this."

Molly closed her eyes and took a deep breath. A sweet smell drifted into her nostrils.

Lilacs, she thought dreamily.

Suddenly Molly's eyes flew open. She sat up ramrod-straight. Something wasn't right. She was no gardener, but she was pretty sure lilac season had ended a long time ago.

Molly shuddered and rubbed her arms. She had the eerie feeling someone else had been in her bed. A creepy thought floated through her mind. Could the lilac be Monsieur Pigot's sickeningly sweet cologne?

A shiver ran up Molly's spine as another possibility—even more frightening—occurred to her.

Or could it be the scent of a ghost?

CHAPTER

The following morning, Molly found her mother at the breakfast table, reading through a stack of newspapers. Molly yawned and leaned down to give her a kiss.

"Morning, Mom." Molly took the opportunity to sniff her mother's perfume. She had hoped it would be lilac today, but it wasn't. Since the night before, she had been smelling lilacs everywhere. But she couldn't figure out where the scent was coming from.

President Wright lowered her newspaper. "Molly, did you just sniff me?"

Molly nodded and sank into her chair next to Jam. It always took her a while to wake up in the morning. "Mom, do you ever wear lilac perfume?"

"No, honey. You know I always wear lily of the valley."

Jam sneezed and pulled on Molly's sleeve. "Mol," he whispered.

Molly jerked her arm away and leaned over the table toward their mother. "Have you noticed everything smells like lilacs lately, Mom?"

"Lilac season was over two months ago," President Wright said, reaching for another newspaper.

"Stop her!" Jam whispered, with urgency this time.

"Cut it out, squirt. I'm thinking." *If it's not Mom, then the lilac smell must be coming from Monsieur Pigot's cologne*, she decided.

Jam tugged so hard on Molly's arm he pinched her skin. Molly was about to turn around and whack him when their mother suddenly leaped up from the table. She held out the newspaper as if it were a snake that might bite her.

"Too late," Jam said, sinking back into his chair.

Molly's eyes fastened on the front section of the *Washington Star*. Splashed across the front page was a blowup of Molly, Jam, and Boomer playing in the Potomac River.

President Wright's voice quavered with anger as she repeated the headline for their benefit. *"President's Kids Escape White House."* She threw it down on the table in front of her children. "Do either of you escapees have anything to say in your defense before I declare punishment?"

Molly considered pleading insanity. After all, they were in the middle of a heatwave with no air conditioning and no water in the White House pools. But one glance at her mother's reddening face and she quickly decided silence was best.

"You are both grounded until further notice. And since I am reasonably certain Molly masterminded this little caper that could have gotten both of you killed, Molly, you will make yourself useful and spend the following week assisting Monsieur Pigot."

Molly groaned and put her head down on the table. Her mother was a master of targeting the most perfect punishment for her children.

"Furthermore," President Wright continued, "both of your allowances are suspended for two weeks."

Jam cried out as if someone had hit him. Molly reached out and gave his arm a reassuring squeeze. She knew there was no punishment more horrible for her money-loving little brother.

"Well, children, was it worth it?" President Wright left them alone to contemplate the answer.

Jam sneezed and wiped his runny nose on his sleeve. "I don't feel so hot," he whined.

But Molly wasn't listening. Her mind was already racing ahead. The ghost had arrived with Monsieur Pigot. Perhaps it would leave with him, too. *The faster he finishes decorating, the faster the ghost will leave*, she reasoned.

Maybe her punishment wasn't such a bad one, after all. She could kill two birds with one stone.

Or in this case, one poltergeist and one very annoying decorator.

*   *   *

Confined to the White House, Molly cheerfully accepted her punishment, convinced that helping Monsieur Pigot would speed his departure, along with the poltergeist's. At first the puzzled decorator was suspicious of her sincerity. But over the next few days, Molly's helpful attitude and hard work convinced him of her change of heart.

Unfortunately, Jam developed a bad cold from their swim in the Potomac River and President Wright left him in Molly's care. Refusing to let his cold slow down their decorating schedule, Molly moved her little brother into the Red Room, where she could keep an eye on him while working.

Molly tapped her foot impatiently as Monsieur Pigot readjusted the Green Room draperies for the third time. He stepped back to check his work. "They're *still* not quite right."

Molly glanced at her Nancy Drew wristwatch. "We've spent forty minutes fiddling with tassels and drapes. If we don't finish the Green Room today, we'll be behind schedule."

"*Schedule.* There's that word again," he said, sinking into a Duncan Phyfe settee. "How many times do I have to tell you, artists do not restrict themselves with schedules, dear girl. Though I must say I am pleased with your attention to detail, there is a fine balance that must be maintained. *Comprenez-vous?*"

Before Molly had a chance to protest, a butler appeared in the doorway carrying a pitcher of iced tea and two glasses on a silver tray. "President Wright thought you might want to take a break for some iced tea with fresh mint from her garden.''

''Lovely! *J'ai soif!*'' Monsieur Pigot clasped his hands together.

''We don't have time for a break,'' Molly insisted. Lunch, or *le déjeuner*, as Monsieur Pigot called it, had been a five-course meal that had lasted almost two hours. At this rate they wouldn't finish until she'd graduated from high school and the poltergeist had completely destroyed her life.

Just then the sound of a bell tinkled from the next room. ''Jam.'' Molly sighed. He had been ringing for her nearly every ten minutes.

''Saved by the bell.'' Monsieur Pigot gestured for the butler to set down the tray. ''Poor little lamb. Your brother needs you, and *I* need this delicious cool glass of iced tea.'' He poured himself a glass and waved her off. ''Go, go!''

Molly found her brother in the Red Room propped up on a mountain of pillows on a sofa Monsieur Pigot had described as ''American Empire.'' Curled up on the floor beside him, Boomer hadn't left Jam's side since he was bedridden. The Red Room had been transformed into a temporary sickroom. Tables were littered with boxes of Kleenex, cough medicine, and glasses of water.

''What is it now?'' Molly glared down at her brother's pale face. He looked even smaller than usual, shivering under a light cotton blanket.

''I'm c-c-c-cold,'' he complained, teeth chattering.

Molly rubbed her arms. That was strange. It *was* surprisingly cool considering D.C. was still in the middle of a record-breaking heatwave. She picked up a paint-splattered dropcloth from the floor and covered her brother with it. As she turned to go, she was called back.

Tinkle, tinkle, tinkle. It was Jam's bell again.

"What now?" she asked, through clenched teeth.

"I'm thirsty."

Molly grabbed a half-empty glass of water smudged with fingerprints from a nearby table and handed it to him.

Jam took a sip and shoved it back at her. "It's warm," he whined, making a face. "That's old water. I want fresh."

"Don't push it, shrimp. I've just about had it with your little-prince routine, ringing for me every two minutes. I'm confiscating your bell. Now go to sleep and stop bugging me. I have work to do. Understand?"

Jam's chin quivered with emotion as he gave a little nod. He reached down and buried his face in Boomer's fur. The faithful Newfoundland seemed to understand and licked the boy's feverish cheeks.

Molly hesitated in the doorway, torn between whether to stay or go. She had tried her best to be sympathetic, but her patience had worn thin. Sometimes she forgot her brother was only seven. She knew it had been particularly hard for him living in the White House. The only ones he could really rely on now were her and Boomer. On the other hand, she had work to do. As long as Monsieur Pigot was there, Molly knew the poltergeist would continue her pranks and she'd keep getting blamed for them.

"I'll read you the financial pages tonight," she promised Jam on her way out. That would be sure to pick up her money-loving brother's spirits. *He'll be okay*, she reassured herself. *He's just tired.*

Molly returned to the Green Room just in time to stop Monsieur Pigot from pouring himself a second glass of iced tea.

"Oh, joy. The slave driver has returned," he said, setting down the pitcher. "What's next on our agenda?"

Molly flipped through her notebook and ran a finger down the list. "Carpets, walls, furniture, draperies . . . here it is, paintings, your favorite."

"Ah, *splendide, peintures.*" Monsieur Pigot seemed to relish rearranging the numerous White House paintings and portraits, endlessly moving them from room to room. They spent the next hour steadily working.

As Molly waited for Monsieur Pigot to make up his mind about the placement of a portrait of President James Madison, she realized how quiet her brother had been.

Too quiet.

She checked her Nancy Drew wristwatch. Jam hadn't rung for her in over an hour. Then Molly noticed the small bell resting on a windowsill and remembered that she had taken it from him. Jam *couldn't* ring for her. An overpowering feeling of dread came over Molly. Something was wrong. Jam was in danger. She could *feel* it.

Suddenly Boomer started barking like crazy, and fear flooded Molly's body.

"What's going on?" the puzzled decorator asked as she bolted from the room.

Molly burst into the Red Room just in time. A heavy marble bust was hovering in midair directly above her brother. Jam stared up at the statue floating over his head, too paralyzed to move.

"Jam!" she shouted, lunging for him.

Jam sat up and cried out in fright just as the marble bust fell.

CHAPTER

7

Molly took a flying leap over the sofa, her hands reaching out to break the statue's fall. She cringed as it grazed Jam's head and hit the floor with a thunderous crash.

Jam fell back with a moan as blood gushed from his forehead. Molly grabbed a pillow and pressed it against the wound to slow the bleeding.

In the next instant, chaos broke loose. Secret Service agents and household staff swarmed into the room.

"What happened?" Roy asked, kneeling to pick up a piece of the broken marble bust. Mike was checking all the windows for signs of intruders and possible break-ins.

At first Molly was too shaken to speak, her throat choked with emotion. "Something fell on him," she whispered. Jam clung to her, sobbing, as she rocked him back and forth, feeling both guilty and scared.

The reason for Jam's complaint about the room being cold was now painfully clear to Molly. It was the unmistakable sign of a ghost's presence—something any amateur ghosthunter would know. But Molly had been too preoccupied to take notice.

She overheard Mike whisper to Roy, "I don't get it. It would take superhuman strength for someone to lift that marble statue alone. How did it get all the way over here from the other side of the room?"

I know, Molly thought, goosebumps dotting her arms.

Boomer whimpered and pushed his nose between Molly and Jam. "Good boy." Jam groaned, reaching out to pet him.

What would have happened if Boomer hadn't barked? Molly wondered. *A split second later the statue would have . . . tears welled up in Molly's eyes as she pushed away the thought. A split second later Jam's skull would have been crushed and he would be lying here dead.*

Molly hugged Jam tight. Tears spilled down her cheeks as she watched the pillow become soaked with her brother's blood.

Suddenly ghosthunting wasn't just a game anymore. She and Jam were in serious danger as long as this poltergeist remained in the White House.

Fear gripped Molly as it never had before.

Was this ghost trying to *kill* them?

That night Molly was still too shaken by the day's events to sleep. Jam had gotten seven stitches on his forehead—one for each year of his life, she had told him. The Secret Service had interrogated Molly about what she had seen until she refused to answer any more questions and pleaded her Fifth Amendment rights. Molly knew that no one had the right to question her legally without her consent.

As soon as Molly could, she contacted Ama on her computer to tell her about the poltergeist's attack. They decided Molly should stop helping Monsieur Pigot so they could concentrate on ghosthunting full-time. That was fine with Molly, since the arrogant decorator had been more concerned with the loss of President Van Buren's antique marble bust than with Jam's near escape from death.

Molly cracked open *The Secret in the Attic* in hopes that rereading her favorite old Nancy Drew mystery would help her relax. But she couldn't get past the first page. *What would Nancy have done if a ghost tried to hurt her brother?* she wondered. But then Nancy Drew didn't have a little brother, and all her mysteries involved tracking down real live criminals, not ghosts. Molly closed her book and kicked back the covers.

"That's it. I can't sit still one second longer." She leaped out of bed and headed for the door. "Back in a second, Ozzie. I'm going to check on Jam."

"Peanut butter and jam! Peanut butter and jam!" the parrot squawked.

It would make the third time tonight she had checked on him. But Molly didn't care if she seemed overprotective. She knew what this poltergeist was capable of and she wasn't taking any chances. She had only one little brother, even if he was a pain in the neck most of the time.

She hurried across the hall and cracked open her brother's bedroom door. By the faint glow of his Rolls-Royce night-light, she could see Jam's arms wrapped around Boomer, both sharing the same pillow. The Newfoundland wasn't allowed up on the furniture, but after the dog helped save Jam's life earlier, Molly had a feeling Boomer would be allowed to do anything he wanted for a while. And Boomer would surely bark again if Jam was in any danger.

Satisfied, Molly shut his door. She was about to return to her bedroom when she heard the faint murmur of voices drifting up the Grand Stairway.

Molly checked her Nancy Drew wristwatch and saw it was 12:06. *Who would have guests at this hour on a Wednesday night?* she wondered. She knew both her parents had gone to bed early, exhausted from Jam's ordeal, and the household staff always took great pains to be quiet.

Perhaps Monsieur Pigot was having a secret late-night party with some of his friends? President Wright had a strict rule that the first-floor staterooms were never to be used for anything but presidential entertaining.

"If I catch *Pig-o* partying in one of the staterooms, Mom will have to dismiss him." Molly ducked into her bedroom for the Instamatic camera in her ghosthunter's backpack. Perhaps she and Jam would be out of danger sooner than she thought. With one photograph she could be rid of Monsieur Pigot *and* the poltergeist forever.

Molly loaded a new roll of film into her camera and crept down the Grand Stairway. She found Mr. Kimmel, the doorman, asleep on a chair in the Entrance Hall. As she tiptoed past him, the voices got louder. They were coming from the Red Room. It sounded like twenty or thirty people talking and laughing. Then she heard the familiar clinking of glasses. *A cocktail party?* she thought. Perhaps she'd get a photo of Monsieur Pigot drunk with a lampshade on his head!

The light was still on in the chief usher's office next to the front door. She saw Mr. Dunbar sitting behind the desk, head down in his work. He often worked late, staying over on a cot in the back of his office.

That's strange, Molly thought. *Why wouldn't Monsieur Pigot have invited Mr. Dunbar to his party?* They had been as inseparable as Siamese twins.

A shiver shot down Molly's spine as she considered another possibility. Perhaps it wasn't a cocktail party that she was hearing. Just two months ago she had stumbled onto a ghostly dinner party hosted by the spirit of President Thomas Jefferson. Ghosts weren't known for photographing well. Still, it was worth a shot.

Clutching her camera, Molly raced across the cold marble floor in her bare feet. A drunk Monsieur Pigot or a partying poltergeist, either way she would have something recorded on film this time.

Molly opened the camera lens and inched along the wall toward the Red Room. "It's now or never," she whispered, taking a deep breath. She stepped into the open doorway, camera raised to her face. "Gotcha!"

What she saw through the camera lens paralyzed her with fear. There was no roomful of people talking and drinking—only one woman dusting a portrait on the wall with a big feather duster.

But it wasn't a White House maid. This woman was wearing an old-fashioned yellow evening gown and a turban with a tall ostrich feather sticking up in front. A cold shiver ran down Molly's back as she recognized the solitary figure.

It was the same woman she had seen walking in the Rose Garden two weeks earlier!

Molly stood motionless, unable to move or breathe as the rest of the scene came into focus. Behind the woman, the walls had turned *yellow* again!

"Get a hold of yourself," Molly whispered, her voice shaking. *The camera must be creating some sort of optical illusion,* she reasoned. Molly slowly lowered the camera as if it were a shield that might protect her.

But the woman was still there, dusting a portrait on the wall—the *yellow* wall.

Molly's mind spun in confusion. Was this real or was she seeing things? She had to know. *If someone doesn't tell me he sees this, too, I'll go crazy,* she thought.

"Mr. Dunbar!" Molly shouted, finding her voice.

She heard his quick steps crossing the marble floor. Finally someone else would verify what she had seen. But as Molly turned back to the room, her heart sank.

The yellow walls had deepened back to crimson red and the woman was gone!

"No one will ever believe me now," she said, staggering into the Red Room. Or was it yellow? She didn't know what she thought anymore. She sank onto the sofa and stared blankly at the large portrait of George Washington the woman had been dusting.

Mr. Dunbar raced into the Red Room. When he saw Molly sitting calmly on the sofa, he breathed a sigh of relief. "I thought I'd find you with your head cracked open like your brother today. Are you out of your mind screaming for me like that?"

Molly nodded in a daze. "I think I *am* out of my mind."

The chief usher gazed intently at her through his thick glasses for a few seconds. "You've seen something, haven't you, Miss Wright?"

Molly looked up at him. She had forgotten Mr. Dunbar was the one adult who might truly understand. As different as they were in temperament, they shared a mutual belief in the supernatural. After all, he had been the first to tell her about the White House's long history of famous ghosts.

"This room keeps changing colors." She waited for him to say she had inhaled too many paint fumes like her mother had suggested. But instead he answered her with another question.

"What color?" he asked with an intensity she hadn't expected.

When Molly answered, "Yellow," one of Mr. Dunbar's eyebrows shot up over his glasses.

"Most interesting," he said thoughtfully. Then, snapping out of his reverie, he added, "There's someone I think you should meet."

Molly watched, puzzled, as Mr. Dunbar walked over to a wall covered with paintings. He pointed up to a portrait of a smiling curly-haired woman.

"Allow me to make the formal introductions, though I suspect you've already made each other's acquaintance tonight. Miss Molly Wright, may I introduce Mrs. Dolley Madison, famous White House hostess and wife of President James—"

"Is she the first lady Dad was reading about who gave so many parties?"

Mr. Dunbar nodded with a grimace. "If you would be so kind as to let me finish without further interruption?"

"Sorry," Molly mumbled, her cheeks turning pink. It was hard keeping quiet when he was so wordy.

"Before this was the Red Room it was known as the Yellow Drawing Room. It was originally decorated in yellow, Dolley's favorite color. So you see, Miss Wright, you may not be as crazy as you think you are."

Molly's mouth hung open in amazement as she watched Mr. Dunbar walk around the room.

"Every Wednesday evening, Dolley Madison threw Washington's most fashionable parties in this very room. You could say she was the original party girl," he said with a chuckle.

But Molly wasn't laughing. *Today is Wednesday,* she realized with a shiver. Goosebumps dotted her arms as she looked around at the red walls that had once been yellow.

"It's hard to imagine the two of you have anything in common," Mr. Dunbar continued. "But she, too, had a pet parrot, as well as a cat named King George."

A cat? Maybe that was what Boomer had been chasing into walls? Molly wondered.

She looked at Dolley's portrait. Something about her seemed familiar. "Did she ever wear turbans with—"

"Feathers?" It was Mr. Dunbar's turn to interrupt. "Dolley often wore turbans with feathered plumes to appear taller. She was self-conscious because she was short."

Molly nodded as the blood drained from her face.

Mr. Dunbar gave a knowing smile. "I *knew* you'd seen her. I take it by your reaction that Dolley Madison has returned to the White House?"

"Yes," Molly whispered. "I mean, I think so."

Mr. Dunbar stared at Molly until she squirmed under his penetrating gaze. "I can't imagine why one of the most famous of all first ladies in White House history would choose to appear to a twelve-year-old

6 8

girl ignorant of her existence," he said, an edge of jealousy in his voice.

With a shrug, as if to say, "There's no accounting for taste," he hurried out of the room as quickly as he had entered it.

Molly's head was spinning. Was the woman who appeared in the Rose Garden and here tonight the ghost of Dolley Madison? She looked at the portrait's cheerful rosy-cheeked face. Could this really be the same woman who tried to hurt Jam?

"What do you want?" Molly whispered. Suddenly Molly felt like a ghost*fighter* instead of a ghosthunter.

Mr. Dunbar had said Dolley was the original party girl. Perhaps she had returned for her father's portrait-unveiling party?

Molly was too tired to think. She decided to sleep on it and consult with Ama in the morning. As she left the Red Room, Molly glanced back up at Dolley's portrait.

A shiver shot up her spine.

She could have sworn she saw Dolley wink.

CHAPTER

8

"I'm positive I sat the portraitist next to Mom." Puzzled, Molly switched the placecards back on a dining table in the State Dining Room. Molly and Ama were helping Mr. Wright with the final preparations for President Wright's upcoming portrait-unveiling party. But someone had been playing musical chairs with their seating arrangements.

"Do you think Dolley did it?" Ama whispered. Molly had told Ama all about her most recent encounter with the first lady the night before.

Molly nodded, "It would be just like her to pull a prank like this."

Just then they heard Jam's voice followed by the sound of paws and feet thundering up the Cross Hall toward the State Dining Room.

"Stop! Boomer! Stop!"

Molly cringed as she heard the unmistakable crash

of glass hitting the floor. In the next instant, Boomer barreled into the dining room with Jam in pursuit.

"Watch out!" Jam warned the girls. But it was too late.

The Newfoundland plowed through a row of chairs, upturning them all. Before Molly and Ama could grab hold of his collar, Boomer's paw caught in the edge of a tablecloth and he pulled down twelve place settings of fine china and crystal.

Molly moaned as she surveyed the wreckage. "Dad's not going to be happy about this."

Boomer crouched on the floor with an apologetic whimper.

"It's okay, boy. We know it's not your fault," Jam said, squatting beside the guilt-ridden dog. "Do you think he's chasing King George again?"

Molly nodded. She had told Ama and Jam about her conversation with Mr. Dunbar last night—Dolley's Yellow Drawing Room, her Wednesday-night parties, and her famous cat, King George.

Jam's face pinched with worry. "We have to tell Mom and Dad the truth. Monsieur Pigot is trying to get them to put Boomer in the kennel."

"The truth? Oh, right, Jam. I can see it now," Ama said, sarcasm creeping into her voice. "President Wright, it wasn't Boomer's fault. He was chasing Dolley Madison's two-hundred-year-old dead cat."

"I see your point," Jam said. Molly gave Jam's shoulder a squeeze. "Don't worry, shrimp. We'll think of something."

Just then Monsieur Pigot burst into the room, followed by President Wright, Mr. Wright, and a small entourage of secretaries. There was a collective gasp as they stopped to take in the disastrous scene.

Monsieur Pigot stepped forward, pointing an accusing finger at Boomer. "See! Didn't I tell you! Look at the damage this animal has caused. He must be put in a kennel. I cannot work with him racing through the house, breaking every priceless artifact in sight."

Jam stood next to the forlorn-looking Newfoundland in a show of solidarity. "If you put Boomer in the kennel, I'll go on a hunger strike. I won't eat anything until I die!"

President Wright slipped an arm around Jam. "Now, now, that's a bit extreme. I think we can come to some fair compromise here."

Monsieur Pigot crossed his arms. "The dog goes or I go."

Jam narrowed his eyes at the decorator. "I'll run away."

President Wright looked at her husband for counsel. But Mr. Wright was still in shock, drifting from one wrecked table to another. "All my careful work ruined," he said, shaking his head in disbelief.

"It's not Boomer's fault," Molly said. "He was chasing something."

"Chasing what?" her mother asked.

Everyone turned to look at Molly. She wanted to tell the truth more than anything. She knew if she

72

didn't, Boomer would get the blame. But just as she was about to spill the beans, Ama shot her a warning look and shook her head with a frown.

"I don't know," Molly said, deflated.

"I do!" Jam piped up, willing to say anything to keep his beloved dog free. "It was a ghost cat!"

All the adults broke into amused grins as a ripple of chuckles went through the room.

President Wright sighed with the weight of her decision. "It's clear something has to be done. Boomer's a good dog and we all love him. But he can't be allowed to destroy the White House and all its treasures. I'm sorry, Jam, but while Monsieur Pigot is still here decorating, Boomer will have to stay outside in the kennel."

Jam opened his mouth to protest, but President Wright raised her hand. "Case closed," she said.

Both Molly and Jam knew this was their mother's final word. No amount of pleading would budge her.

"Come on, boy. We're leaving," Jam said, his eyes downcast. Boomer looked up at Jam, ready to follow him anywhere. On the way out, Jam paused by Monsieur Pigot and narrowed his eyes. "This is war," he said and bolted from the room with Boomer lumbering after him.

When President Wright turned to go, Monsieur Pigot cleared his throat. "Excuse me, Madam President. I hate to be a bother when you've been so helpful, but I'm afraid I have to mention another unpleasant matter. Every morning the Gilbert Stuart portrait of George Washington, which I've displayed in the Red Room, keeps mysteriously turning up in the East Room." His eyes wandered over to Molly, placing silent blame.

"That's not fair! I didn't do it!" Molly knew it was Dolley working her mischief again. But she wasn't going to make the same mistake Jam did. Talk about invisible ghost cats was cute coming from a seven-year-old, but she knew her mother would think otherwise if Molly blamed the roving portrait on a poltergeist.

President Wright rubbed her forehead as if this was all giving her a giant headache. "What do you propose, Monsieur Pigot?"

The decorator leaned forward, smiling smoothly. "Perhaps it would be less tempting for the children if we simply put it in storage?"

"Fine. Do it," President Wright said, eager to be done with the matter.

When everyone had left the dining room, Ama checked her watch. "Sorry to leave you with this mess, Mol, but—"

"I know, I know," Molly said with a sigh. "You've got to go home and babysit Kena."

Ama nodded with a shrug, as if to say, "What can I do?" She started making a path through the debris of broken dishes to the door.

"I'll walk you downstairs," Molly offered, hurrying after her.

Suddenly Molly heard the unmistakable sound

of another dish crashing to the floor and spun around.

No one was there.

That night, Molly sat on the new, ridiculously-frilly computer chair Mr. Pigot had put in her room, typing out another Ghost Report. By the time she'd finished, she was fuming mad.

"I'm getting sick and tired of Dolley's ghost playing games at my expense," she said to Ozzie, who was perched on top of her computer monitor. "Can you believe she and that ghost cat had the gall to wreck Dad's dinner-party tables and get Boomer put in the clinker?"

The parrot rose up and flapped her wings in outrage.

"And then she gets me blamed again for moving some dumb portrait around. If anyone had stopped to think, they would have realized a twelve-year-old girl couldn't move a portrait that big by herself. The frame alone must weigh over a hundred pounds."

Molly turned off the computer and flung herself across her bed, wallowing in self-pity. "I'm the only one in this house with any kind of deductive reasoning," she whispered into her pillow.

Just then she heard two short raps followed by a knock on her door. It was Jam's secret code. "Come in!" she shouted.

Jam entered wearing a raincoat and hat. He held

a small battery-operated television in one hand and Boomer's favorite rag-doll toy in the other.

"What's with the raingear, Jam?"

"It's raining," he said.

"So?"

"I'm sleeping in the kennel with Boomer."

Molly simply nodded. She knew there was no use in trying to talk him out of it. Her brother had been inseparable from Boomer since he was born.

Jam padded over to her bed in his rain boots. He lowered his face so close to hers that she could smell the peanut butter on his breath. "I've got some dirt on Pigot," he whispered.

Molly raised up on one elbow. If anyone had more reason than she did to hate Pigot, it was Jam. She could see the anger flash in his eyes. "Well? Spill the beans, Sherlock."

Jam took a quick glance around the room to make sure no one was listening. "He says he's from Washington, D.C., but his license plate is from Rhode Island."

Molly fell back on her bed and stared up at the ceiling. What could she expect from a seven-year-old amateur? "So what, Jam?" she said. "Maybe he bought his car in another state."

Jam shook his head. "It's a phony. I checked it out. Rhode Island license plates say Ocean State, but his says Vacationland. That's Maine."

Molly nodded, not knowing what to make of it.

Jam glanced at her clock. "I've gotta go. *Lifestyles*

of the Rich and Famous comes on in five minutes. Can I borrow a pillow?''

"Sure." Molly stuffed one under his arm and escorted him to the door.

" 'Hope,' " Jam said over his shoulder on the way out. Before Molly had a chance to ask what he meant, he explained, "Rhode Island's state motto."

"Mine, too," Molly whispered, closing the door behind him. But the truth was, she was beginning to lose all hope. It had been over two weeks since she saw Dolley's ghost in the Rose Garden and she still didn't know what the mischievous first lady wanted.

"I'm starving," she said to Ozzie as she put him back in his cage. Realizing she had been too upset to even touch her dinner that night, Molly decided to go downstairs to the kitchen for a snack. Gisella, the head chef, often left late-night snacks in the refrigerator for Molly and Mr. Wright, the resident night owls.

On her way downstairs, Molly found Monsieur Pigot still at work in the Red Room. He was supervising some houseman on the removal of the enormous portrait of George Washington. Just the sight of the decorator made Molly's blood boil. *Because of him, Jam and Boomer are sleeping in the kennel and I'm in the doghouse with Mom and Dad*, she thought, marching over to give him a piece of her mind.

"I hope you're happy now that you've gotten what you wanted, Monsieur *Pig-o*." She waited for him to flinch at the gross mispronunciation of his name, but he didn't.

"Thank you for your concern, Miss Wright," he said with a smug grin. "In fact, I *am* very happy this evening." He turned his back to her and continued working.

After grabbing a bagel from the kitchen, Molly stomped upstairs and slammed the door to her bedroom shut so hard Ozzie squawked "Abandon ship!" for three minutes straight.

That night, an eerie silence hung over the White House.

The following day, Molly was determined to figure out why Dolley Madison had returned to the White House. But again, it was too hot to investigate during the day. Besides, Molly knew ghosthunting during daylight hours was a waste of time. Ghosts almost always chose to appear at night.

Perhaps Ama would have some thoughts on the matter when she slept over that night, Molly hoped. She couldn't wait for her best friend to arrive. She loved their sleepovers; trying new hairstyles, eating popcorn and watching videos, and best of all, ghosthunting. It almost made up for not having a sister.

It seemed like the long hot day would never end. Molly almost wished Dolley would play another of her mischievous pranks on her to liven things up. Ever since Molly had run into Monsieur Pigot removing the portrait the previous night, everything had been so quiet.

Too quiet.

That night, behind closed doors, Molly and Ama read through all of Molly's Ghost Reports, trying to find a reason for the first lady's return. But they came up empty-handed.

"We don't have enough clues," Ama said, holding up a hand mirror to check the back of her new stylish bun. They had both tried new hairstyles from a fashion magazine Ama had brought over.

"I give up." Molly flopped down on her bed, sending a dozen long skinny braids flying into the air around her head. One braid landed over her eye. She lifted it and looked at Ama. "Want to take Boomer for a walk on the South Lawn? At least it's cooler outside."

What Molly didn't say was that she had promised Jam she would take care of Boomer while he was sick. Jam's rainy night in the kennel had worsened his cold and their mother had insisted he stay in bed.

"Sure," Ama said. "Then we can watch this video I brought." She held up a tape of *Ghostbusters.*

They found the lethargic Newfoundland sprawled out across the floor of the kennel. Molly clapped her hands together. "Want to go for a walk, boy?" she asked enthusiastically.

Boomer opened one eye, looked at her, and closed it again.

"What's wrong with him?" Ama asked.

"He misses Jam," Molly explained, clipping a leash to the dog's collar. "My brother's the same way without Boomer. It's pathetic."

The girls had barely stepped out of the kennel when Boomer lifted his head, ears perked. Suddenly he lunged forward, straining hard against the leash.

"Stop it, Boomer!" Molly grabbed the leash with both hands and pulled back with all her might. Ama tried to help her, but it was no use. The leash slid through their hands, and Boomer tore off across the South Lawn.

"What's he chasing?" Ama asked. "I didn't see anything." But as soon as the words were out of her mouth, she turned to Molly. "You don't think it was—"

"Dolley's cat?" Molly said, finishing her friend's thought.

Without another word, the girls took off across the lawn after the running dog. By the time they caught up with Boomer in the Rose Garden, he had trampled the gardener's newly-planted begonias. Molly found him panting in a heap on top of some squashed daisies.

"Sorry, Tony." Molly tiptoed past the irritated gardener into the ruined flowerbed. "Bad dog," she whispered, slipping the leash back on Boomer's collar.

Boomer gave a little whimper and licked her hand. Molly's anger dissolved as she gave his head a pat. "Okay, okay, I know it wasn't your fault." Boomer leaped up and followed her onto the grass, his tail wagging.

Molly paused by the gardener. "It's a pretty garden," she said, trying to make up for what happened.

"It *was* pretty." Tony picked up the uprooted begonias, one by one, and tossed them in his wheelbarrow.

"Back in Ghana, my mother used to do all her gardening at night," Ama said, leaning over to smell a rose. "It was the only time cool enough to enjoy it. She said the plants enjoyed it more then, too." She looked up at Tony with her big brown eyes and gave him a heartwarming smile.

Tony couldn't resist smiling back. "Your mother was right. Night's the best time to garden." Hooking his thumbs through the straps of his overalls, he closed his eyes and inhaled the night air. "Even smells better."

Suddenly it occurred to Molly that Tony might know where the lilac smell was coming from. If anyone knew, he would. He had been head gardener at the White House for thirty-five years. "Tony, do you know where the lilac bushes are?" she asked.

Tony grabbed the handles of his wheelbarrow, ready to push off. "There haven't been any lilacs on this lawn since old President Madison. They were his wife's favorite flower. I guess she even wore lilac water all the time. It was her . . . what do you ladies call it?"

Ama leaned forward. "Her signature scent?"

"Yep, that's it." Tony touched the brim of his hat in a parting gesture and guided the wheelbarrow back to the greenhouse.

Molly's eyes met Ama's as they both whispered the same word: *"Dolley."*

Molly swallowed hard and said in a hushed tone, "Every time I smelled lilacs, Dolley's ghost must have been watching me."

Ama for once had nothing to say. She could only gaze consolingly at her friend, as a cold shiver rolled down Molly's back.

CHAPTER

9

On their way back to Molly's bedroom, the girls heard someone sniffling.

"It better not be Jam," Molly said, pausing on the first-floor stairway to listen. "Mom will kill him if he got out of bed with a fever."

"Shhhh." Ama held a finger to her lips, her brow furrowed in concentration. "It sounds like somebody's crying."

The girls went back down the stairs and followed the sound across the Entrance Hall toward the staterooms.

"I think it's coming from the Red Room," Molly whispered, leading the way. As she crept toward the open door, the heart-wrenching sobs got louder. It *was* someone crying.

Molly crouched by the doorway as the two girls peered around the corner into the Red Room. They gasped at what they saw.

A small woman wearing an old-fashioned yellow evening gown was sitting on the sofa, dabbing her eyes with a lace handkerchief. She stared at a blank spot on the wall as if heartbroken.

Ama clutched Molly's hand. "Is it *her?*" she whispered.

Molly nodded, dumbstruck. Dolley's ghost had never seemed so *real* before. Or so vulnerable. Could this possibly be the same woman who hurt Jam with the statue? One look at her face and Molly *knew* Dolley would never intentionally harm anyone. Soft black curls framed a sweet face with a heartbreakingly sad expression.

"She's fading," Ama whispered.

In the next instant, Dolley was gone. For almost a full minute, neither of the girls could speak.

As Molly stepped into the room, she noticed the scent of lilacs still lingered in the air. She touched the spot on the sofa where Dolley had sat just moments before. "I wonder why she was crying?" she whispered, sitting down.

Ama tentatively followed her into the room. "It's hard to believe she was the same ghost who hurt Jam."

Molly tried to rub away the goosebumps dotting her arms. "I don't think she meant to hurt him. She was just trying to get my attention."

Ama sat down beside Molly. "The question is, *why* was she trying to get your attention?"

Both girls stared straight ahead at the blank spot on the wall where Dolley had been looking.

Suddenly Ama straightened up. "You said Pigot has been constantly changing furniture around, right?"

Molly nodded, still touched by Dolley's melancholy.

"Paintings, too?"

Molly nodded, wondering where her friend's line of questioning was leading.

Ama pointed straight ahead to the blank spot on the wall where Dolley had been staring. "Was anything hanging there before?"

Molly thought back to the night before, when she found Monsieur Pigot moving a large portrait off that very spot on the wall. "A big portrait of George Washington was there," she said, turning toward Ama as another thought occurred to her. "That was the *same* portrait Dolley was dusting when I found her in here the last time."

Molly's eyes met Ama's for a brief second.

Ama was already halfway to the door. "Come on! We've got research to do! The portrait's the clue we've been looking for!"

Molly switched on her computer as Ama jammed a chair against the bedroom door to make sure no one entered unexpectedly.

"Log on to the Internet, run the Web Browser and type in *www.loc.gov.* for the Library of Congress," Ama instructed, leaning over Molly's shoulder.

"I *know* how to do it," Molly said, unable to keep the irritation out of her voice. Ama could be so bossy sometimes. Just because she was a computer whiz, she acted like everyone else didn't know how to turn one on.

Both girls were silent as a picture of the magnificent old library appeared on the computer screen.

"First we need to find out about the portrait of George Washington," Molly said, typing in the name of its painter, Gilbert Stuart. She remembered Monsieur Pigot mentioning his name several times.

"*And* why the portrait meant so much to Dolley," Amy added.

Molly glanced over her shoulder at Ama and smiled. They were working like a team now. A ghosthunter team.

"Scoot over," Ama said, squeezing in beside Molly on the chair. Together, they silently read the information as it appeared on the computer screen:

"Gilbert Stuart's 1797 full-length portrait of George Washington is the oldest object in the White House. It is the only object to have survived the War of 1812, when the portrait was rescued by Dolley Madison shortly before the British burned the White House on August 24, 1814.

Dolley Madison had refused to abandon the portrait though her own life was in peril. With just two scant hours before the British arrived, Dolley ordered the portrait's frame broken and the canvas taken out. She left it in the hands of two gentlemen from New York for safekeeping and fled the White House disguised as a peasant woman to avoid being taken prisoner by the British army.

Her efforts were successful as the portrait was returned to the White House when it was later rebuilt.

On that hot fateful day of August 24, 1814, with her husband, President James Madison, away and only a few men standing between the White House and the enemy, Dolley writes to her sister: ". . . I am still here, within sound of the cannons! Mr. Madison comes not: may God protect him! Two messengers, covered with dust, come to bid me fly; but I wait for him . . .

"Our kind friend, Mr. Carroll, has come to hasten my departure, and is in a very bad humor with me because I insist on waiting until the large picture of General Washington is secured, and it requires to be unscrewed from the wall. This process was found too tedious for these perilous moments! I have ordered the frame to be broken, and the canvas taken out: it is done—and the precious portrait placed in the hands of two gentlemen from New York for safekeeping. And now, dear sister, I must leave this house . . . When I shall again write to you, or where I shall be tomorrow, I cannot tell!!"

"Wow." Molly slouched in front of the computer screen, imagining the dramatic scene: The brave first lady saving Washington's portrait and narrowly escaping the British invasion as the White House went up in flames behind her.

Equally impressed, Ama sank back, shaking her head in amazement. "No wonder Dolley was crying. It must be really upsetting to see some silly decorator moving around a portrait you've risked your life to save. I feel sorry for her, don't you?"

Molly reluctantly nodded in agreement. She had to admit her feelings toward the mischievous first lady were softening. It was hard to still feel angry now that she understood Dolley's courageous role in the portrait's dramatic rescue so many years ago.

Ama leaped up and began pacing the floor, anxious to get back to work. "The question is, why did she appear to us tonight?"

Molly shrugged. "I guess she knows we're detectives," she said, following Ama's line of thought. "She must have figured we'd find out about her connection to Washington's portrait."

Ama held up a finger to make a point. "But why was she so upset about it being moved? Didn't Pigot just leave it in storage temporarily until he decides where to put it?"

"Maybe we should check on it for Dolley just to make sure it's okay?" Molly suggested.

"I guess so. After all, we're Dolley's detectives

now," Ama said, bending her knees and doing an old-fashioned curtsy.

"Let's check *Pig-o's* studio first," Molly said, heading for the door. "He keeps a lot of stuff in there."

But the girls found the decorator's studio locked. Too late to investigate any further, they decided to continue their search after the presidential portrait-unveiling party the following night.

Back in Molly's bedroom, Ama brushed her teeth while Molly slipped on her FBI "Ten Most Wanted" nightshirt. Ama had one just like it that she wore whenever they had a sleepover. As she struggled to pull on her nightshirt, Molly smiled at the thought of watching *Ghostbusters* and eating popcorn in bed with her best friend. With a final yank, Molly's head popped out.

Molly gasped, staring at what she saw before her.

Just a few feet away, Dolley Madison was sitting in her bed! And she was eating what looked like a big dish of *ice cream!*

Then Ama walked in from the bathroom, brushing her hair, oblivious to her paralyzed friend. "Let's eat something different this time," she said. "I'm sick of popcorn."

Speechless, Molly glanced at Ama and then back at Dolley.

But Dolley had disappeared!

"Br-r-r. It's freezing in here," Ama said, rubbing her arms as she sat down on the bed, where Dolley had been only seconds before. "Did the air conditioning just go on?"

When Molly didn't answer, Ama looked at her pale-faced friend. "What's wrong? You look as if you've just seen a"—Ama sniffed the lilac-scented air, her eyes widening with the realization of what had happened.

"A ghost," Molly whispered, finishing Ama's sentence for her.

Ama rushed to her side. "Was it Dolley?"

Unable to speak another word, Molly just pointed to her bed.

Ama went over to where she pointed and picked up a dish of ice cream with two spoons sticking out of it. "Great! You ordered ice cream. Much better than popcorn." She took a bite and closed her eyes. "M-m-m-m," she said, savoring the delicious creamy flavor. She offered Molly the other spoon. "You know, I read somewhere that Dolley Madison introduced ice cream to the White House. Did you know it was one of her favorite desserts at parties?"

Still stunned, Molly dipped a spoon into the ghostly dish of ice cream and took a bite.

The cold sweetness slithered down her throat.

Dolley was depending on them.

CHAPTER

10

Finally the night of the presidential portrait-unveiling party arrived. The *Washington Post* hailed it as "the social event of the summer," and the guest list of over one hundred prominent Washington, D.C., socialites and artists had been released to the press.

Molly, Ama, and Jam were invited to attend the portrait unveiling in the East Room after the guests had finished with cocktails and dinner. And Ama had agreed to sleep over so they could continue their search for the missing portrait later that night.

Molly dropped by her parents' bedroom before the guests arrived to see how her father was holding up. She found Mr. Wright fumbling nervously with his bow tie in front of the dressing-room mirror.

"Opening-night jitters, Dad?" Molly stood on her tiptoes and reached up to straighten his lopsided bow tie.

Mr. Wright took a deep breath and smiled, putting

on a brave front. He held up both hands and crossed his fingers. "Wish me luck, Mol. Everything's running like clockwork so far. I've consulted my astrological chart and the planets are all in perfect alignment tonight."

"That's great, Dad." Molly knew her father had been frantically checking and rechecking every party detail for days, making sure his social debut as White House host and first husband ran as smoothly as possible.

"Is that you, Molly?" President Wright swept into the room, relaxed and radiant in a full-length yellow satin evening gown.

"You look awesome, Mom." Molly couldn't help thinking how Dolley would approve of her mother's choice of color.

Mr. Wright rushed forward to give his wife a hug and a kiss. "You're pretty as a picture," he said, beaming at her, still clearly in love.

"I hope so," she said, glancing in the mirror with a sigh. "Especially since all our guests will be comparing me to my portrait tonight."

"Shall we go, Madam President?" Mr. Wright extended an elbow. President Wright slipped a gloved hand through his arm and they walked out.

Molly followed her parents to the top of the Grand Stairway. As the United States Marine Band struck up "Hail to the Chief," she watched them descend the stairs together. She had seen it dozens of times before, but the moment never seemed to lose its magic.

It was nearly ten o'clock by the time all the guests had finished dinner and moved into the East Room for the official portrait unveiling.

President Wright, the portraitist, and Mr. Rexon, the head of the White House Historical Association, stood on a platform at the far end of the cavernous East Room. The covered portrait rested on an easel beside them.

Molly, Ama, and Jam were led to the front of the crowd, where Mr. Wright was standing. Molly beamed with pride at her mother on the stage. Most of the time, she hated being the first daughter, like at school and in public when total strangers stared at her, but at times like this, she felt important.

Molly gave her father's jacket sleeve a tug. "How's it going?" she whispered.

"So far, so good." Mr. Wright showed her his hidden crossed fingers.

Ama nudged Molly. "What's *he* doing here?" She glanced back over her shoulder. Standing directly behind them was Monsieur Pigot. He nodded at them with a smug grin. Just looking at him made her blood boil. She turned back around as the portrait-unveiling ceremony began.

Mr. Rexon took center stage. "President Wright, Mr. Wright, ladies and gentlemen, as you know, we are here this evening to witness the official unveiling of President Wright's portrait, which will soon take its place in history among . . ."

Molly's mind wandered as the speaker droned on

about history, her least favorite subject. She rubbed the goosebumps on her arms. *They must have turned on the air conditioning for the ceremony,* she thought. But then she looked up at her father's perspiring forehead and noticed several people fanning themselves with their programs.

What was going on?

Molly answered her own question as she felt a familiar supernatural presence in the room. Ama gave Molly a nudge. As their eyes met, Molly knew Ama felt it, too.

Suddenly Molly had an overwhelming feeling of dread, the *same* feeling she had had just before the marble bust fell on Jam. Trouble was brewing, and Molly was sure Dolley was behind it.

Molly's eyes darted around the room. Was her mother in danger as Jam had been? Squinting into the bright light, she looked up at the gigantic crystal chandelier hanging directly above the platform where her mother stood. Were the small gleaming bits of cut glass shaking? Or was it her imagination? Molly's entire body tightened with fear. Her parents and everyone would think she had lost her mind if she told them what she suspected.

Maybe she was wrong, but she couldn't take that risk.

Molly opened her mouth, ready to shout for her mother to jump to safety, when she caught something flickering out of the corner of her eye. On the wall to one side of the platform, long heavy damask draperies hung to the floor. Suddenly a small flame raced up along one edge and licked the ceiling.

Before Molly could draw a breath, someone yelled, "Fire!" The entire curtain went up in a wall of flames!

In the next instant, Secret Service agents swarmed the East Room, lifting President Wright off the stage. Mike grabbed Molly and pushed her through the stampeding crowd for one of the doors.

"Dad!" Molly cried, twisting her body around to look back for her family. But Secret Service agents had already whisked them away. She didn't see Ama anywhere, either.

As guests ran screaming from the room, Molly took one last look back. Secret Service agents had already torn down the curtains and were stamping out the flames.

"Darn candles," Mike muttered, pushing Molly out through the door.

That's strange, Molly thought. *The candlelight sconces on the wall were nowhere near those curtains.*

"Dolley," Molly said angrily. It had to be another one of her pranks.

"Did you say something?" Mike guided Molly into the First Family's private elevator and pressed *2*.

Molly just shook her head, her mind racing. What could possibly be so important to Dolley that she was willing to set the White House on fire to get her attention?

Molly shivered with fear.

She knew if she didn't figure it out soon, someone would *really* get hurt next time.

Later that night, Molly and Ama sat up in bed trying to figure out why Dolley had pulled such a dangerous prank.

"It's hard to believe she'd actually set fire to her old house," Ama said, "especially after the British burned down the White House when she lived here."

Frustrated, Molly punched one of her pillows. "She must have been *really* desperate to get our attention this time."

Finally they decided to make a list of Dolley's pranks and ghost sightings. "Maybe we'll see a pattern," Molly reasoned.

Ama grabbed a pen and paper. "I'm game. This has to be about more than Dolley being mad that her favorite portrait was moved."

Molly quickly agreed and they set to work on their list:

Dolley's Ghost Sightings and Pranks

1. *Dolley in Rose Garden with cat*
   —angry about Molly messing with her roses?
2. *Keeps moving Pig-o's furniture/paintings back*
   —wants to drive Pig-o crazy?
   —doesn't like his decorating?
   —wants to get Molly in trouble?
3. *Breaks vase in East Room*

—she's a music critic/thinks Molly's piano play-ing stinks?
—wants to get Molly in trouble **again?**
4. *Drops marble statue on Jam*
   —doesn't like sick little kids?
   —doesn't want Jam getting germs all over her Red/Yellow Room?
5. *Turns Red Room yellow and back again*
   —wants to drive Molly crazy?
   —showing off?
6. *Makes Boomer chase invisible ghost cat*
   —she's a cat lover/hates dogs?
   —wants to have a good laugh?
7. *Turns flowers into goldenrod*
   —thinks it's funny to make Pig-o sneeze? (It is)
   —wants to get Molly in trouble **again?**
8. *Plays musical chairs with seating arrangements*
   —wants to wreck Mr. Wright's party?
   —she's jealous/doesn't want Mr. Wright to be a better hostess than she was?
9. *Eats ice cream in Molly's bed*
   —wanted to overhear us talk about her?
   —wants to scare us
   —wants to get us fat?
10. *Sets fire to curtains*
    —wants to ruin Mr. Wright's first party?
    —wants to get our attention!

Molly read through the list and sighed. "This doesn't add up to anything but a lot of mischief. I'm beginning to think female ghosts are nothing but trouble.''

Ama picked up *The Secret in the Attic* on Molly's bedside table and said, "I wonder what Nancy would do."

Molly knew she meant Nancy Drew. They both shared a real love and admiration for the resourceful heroine in the mystery series. "How about a little old-fashioned investigating?" she said, grabbing her flashlight and heading for the door.

Ama didn't have to be asked twice. She was right behind Molly. They both knew it was the perfect time to investigate—after midnight, when everyone would be in bed, fast asleep.

Except for ghosts.

Molly and Ama crept into the pitch-black East Room guided by a narrow shaft of light. A strong smell of smoke still hung in the air. Without a word, the girls headed for the window where the curtain had gone up in flames just hours before. They searched for the burned curtains, but they were gone.

"The maids must have taken the curtains away already," Ama said, disappointed. "How are we supposed to get any investigating done around here when the White House staff is always cleaning up all our evidence?"

Molly didn't answer. She was examining the bare window for clues. She directed the flashlight along the white wall that had turned black with smoke damage. "They sure didn't clean the walls yet," Molly said, running the light along the blackened wall. Her hand froze as the light shone on a big perfect rectangle of white, about five feet from the floor. It was the *only* spot untouched by smoke damage.

"How did that happen?" Ama whispered over her shoulder. "I don't remember any picture hanging here before the fire."

"That's because there *wasn't* anything here before." Molly felt a chill shoot through her as she realized what was happening. "Dolley's giving us a clue," she whispered, almost afraid to say it out loud. An idea was taking shape in her mind, and she bolted for the door.

"Hey, where are you going?" Ama said, racing after Molly. "You've got the flashlight! Don't leave me in the dark!"

But Molly wasn't waiting for anyone. She had to find out if her hunch was right. Ama caught up with Molly back in her bedroom, rummaging through her desk. "My inventory notebook," she said, pulling it out of a drawer. "I kept it when I worked with Pig-o. Every move he made is in here." She flipped through the pages. "East Room, here it is." She ran a finger down the page. "East wall by window . . . I knew it."

"Knew *what?*" Ama said, ready to shake her.

"Gilbert Stuart's portrait of George Washington hung on that wall. I knew it had been there before Pig-o moved it to the Red Room."

"And then he moved it again into storage," Ama

added. "You know, that portrait must be pretty valuable if it's the oldest object in the whole White
House."

Molly and Ama's eyes met.

"The portrait's in danger," Molly whispered.
"That's what Dolley's been trying to tell us all along."

CHAPTER

11

The following day, Molly woke in the dark early morning hours to her bedside lamp flicking on and off. She reached over and turned off the lamp. But it seemed to have a mind of its own, going right back on and then flickering some more.

"Come on, Mol. Stop playing games," Ama moaned, still half-asleep. She covered her head with a pillow.

"I'm not doing it," Molly said, knowing there was no use in unplugging it. Dolley would just continue playing her game.

Ama's eyes snapped open as she realized what was happening. "Dolley?"

Molley sat up in bed and stretched her arms. "Yep. It's just her little way of saying she doesn't want her detectives sleeping on the job."

Ama clung to her pillow. "I thought ghosts were only supposed to come out at night."

Molly spoke to the flickering lamp. "Okay, Dolley, I'm awake. You've got my attention. You want me working at the crack of dawn to track down your portrait? Fine. On one condition. No more pranks. Understand?"

The bedside lamp went off. And stayed off.

Molly smiled triumphantly. She flipped back the sheets and leaped out of bed. "Come on lazybones," she said, giving Ama's inert body a shove. "We've got work to do."

Molly and Ama quickly dressed and grabbed a bite in the Family Dining Room. They found Mr. Wright hunched over the table, sipping coffee and staring into space.

"Why are you up so early, Dad?" When Molly planted a kiss on his cheek, Mr. Wright seemed to wake up out of a trance.

"Oh, good morning, girls," he said, forcing a smile as he held up the newspaper. "See today's paper, yet? Your old dad's famous, or rather, infamous."

Molly leaned over and read the headline out loud, *"First Husband's Party Goes up in Smoke."* As she looked at her dejected father, she bristled with the knowledge that Dolley had ruined his first White House party with one of her pranks. Molly knew how much it had meant to him. He looked so miserable, she couldn't resist trying to cheer him up.

"Look at it this way, Dad. At least no one will ever *forget* your party."

Ama nodded in agreement as they grabbed a couple of muffins and left Mr. Wright to ponder the thought.

As soon as the girls stepped off the elevator onto the first floor, they heard Monsieur Pigot's voice. They followed it into the East Room, where they found him mourning the loss of the curtains with Mr. Dunbar.

"They were exquisite, one of a kind," the decorator said. "You can't find French damask like that anymore. Hand-stitched, old-world craftsmanship. And now they're gone forever. *Finis!*"

"Who died?" Molly asked, appearing in the doorway.

Startled, Monsieur Pigot clutched his chest. "I would appreciate it if you would announce your arrival, Miss Wright. I am not accustomed to eavesdroppers."

Molly marched straight up to him. She had one burning question to ask and it couldn't wait—Dolley might pull another dangerous prank, and she couldn't take that risk. "Where did you put the portrait of George Washington?"

Monsieur Pigot seemed stricken by the question. He forced a laugh. "I really don't know what you mean by *the* portrait. President Washington was a very famous man. He had many portraits painted of him." He turned around, dismissing her.

Ama nudged Molly and glanced up at the smoke-damaged wall where the clean white rectangle had been. It was gone!

Molly felt as if it were a sign from Dolley. The first lady was finally through with playing games. She must have realized that Molly understood, at last, what she had been trying to communicate.

Molly walked around to face Monsieur Pigot. "Let me refresh your memory. I'm talking about his most famous portrait. The one you kept moving around. It was here in the Red Room and now it's in storage somewhere. Where is it exactly?"

Mr. Dunbar stepped forward, indignant. "Really, Miss Wright. You may be the president's daughter, but that gives you no call to be rude."

Molly ignored him. "I need to update my inventory. Where is it, Monsieur Pigot?"

The decorator's face drained of color. "I really don't remember. I can't be expected to keep track of every little detail. Now, if you'll excuse me, I have work to do."

"Fine," Molly said, narrowing her eyes at him. "I'll just tell Mom you forgot where the White House's oldest, most valuable artifact is." As she turned to go, Monsieur Pigot's hand reached out to stop her.

"Don't be silly. You're making such a fuss over nothing. It's no secret. I believe it's in the third-floor storage room. Be my guest." He handed her a key.

"*Merci*," Ama said, just before they raced out of the room.

"We'll never find it in here. It's too dark," Molly said, knocking her knee into a box. She shone the flashlight on it and read, IKE AND MAMIE'S CHINA. She had never seen so much old stuff. The storage room was gigantic and packed to the rafters with boxes. The girls had been searching for the portrait in the hot dark room for nearly two hours.

"You'd think it would be easy to find," Ama said. "After all, the portrait's larger than life-size."

Molly was ready to give up. "I guess Pigot wouldn't have given us the key if he had anything to hide. Let's go. It's boiling in here."

Just then a high-pitched *yowl* pierced the air.

Molly froze as a chill rolled down her back.

It sounded *inhuman*.

Ama leaped over a pile of boxes and crouched next to her friend. "What was that?" she whispered, huddling close.

Molly held her breath and listened, too scared to move. A soft meowing sound was coming from the far corner. Molly slowly moved her flashlight across the room. She stopped, paralyzed by what she saw.

Two glowing round green eyes stared back at her.

The *same* green eyes that had stared back at her once before.

"It's Dolley's cat," Molly whispered, her hand shaking. When she managed to steady the light, the cat had vanished!

"Hey, Mol, look at this." Ama moved over to the corner where the cat had been and looked at a huge sealed crate. She tried to pry it open with her bare hands, but it was firmly nailed shut. "Isn't this

1 0 5

big enough to hold that portrait?'' Ama asked excitedly.

"I guess so.'' Molly couldn't think straight. The air was thick with the sickeningly sweet smell of lilacs. It was so stuffy she couldn't breathe. She felt woozy. The walls started to close in on her.

Suddenly a burst of frigid air encircled Molly's body and a roller-coaster shiver raced up her spine.

Molly bolted for the door. "I've got to get out of here!''

Molly felt like her old self once she had a cold soda and sat down in her room for a while. "I'm okay. The heat just got to me,'' she assured Ama before her friend agreed it would be best to leave her and go home.

"I just needed a little rest,'' Molly said to herself after seeing Ama out. She sat down at her computer, ready to start work again.

Jam's theory about Pigot's license plate kept running through her mind. She had a nagging feeling that the answer was within her reach, though it kept eluding her. But one thing she'd learned as a ghosthunter was that no clue was too small to follow up.

Molly switched on the computer and ran Pigot's license-plate numbers through the Department of Motor Vehicles. There was no match in the DMV files, however. "The DMV doesn't lie,'' Molly said, staring at the screen. "But apparently Monsieur Pigot does.''

Something didn't add up. Why would a decorator bother to get a phony license plate? He didn't exactly conjure up the image of a typical criminal. Molly grinned at the thought of Monsieur Pigot in his get-away car, wearing a beret with his scarf flying out behind him.

"It's too ridiculous," Molly said, shaking her head and switching off the computer. Still, she couldn't shake a feeling of dread that had hung over her all day. "I'm probably just hungry," she said, heading for the door. In all the excitement, she hadn't eaten anything but half a muffin since breakfast.

On her way to the kitchen, Molly passed Mr. Dunbar sitting on a chair in the hall, staring into space. She almost didn't recognize him. She couldn't remember ever seeing the energetic Mr. Dunbar when he wasn't in motion.

"What's wrong, Mr. Dunbar? You look like you've just lost your best friend?" Molly braced herself for his usual sarcastic answer.

"Precisely," he said with a sigh. His expression clouded over as he turned to her. "You'll be pleased to know that Monsieur Pigot has finished his work here sooner than expected."

"That's too bad. When's he leaving?" Molly tried to keep the enthusiasm out of her voice for Mr. Dunbar's sake, but it was impossible. The decorator had made her life miserable.

"This afternoon," Mr. Dunbar said, his voice crack-

1 0 7

ing with emotion. The chief usher leaped to his feet and hurried down the hall.

Molly found piles of suitcases and boxes marked PIGOT at the top of the Grand Stairway. *Probably full of his stupid paint chips and fabric swatches,* she thought, squeezing past a huge crate.

"Wait a minute." Molly ran a hand over the familiar-looking crate. It was the same one from the storage room, the one Ama had tried to pry open. She paused for a moment, trying to see inside, but it was sealed tight, and besides, Molly was hungry. She had an uneasy feeling as she walked down the stairs.

"Boomer! Stop!" It was Jam's voice.

"Not again," Molly groaned as the Newfoundland bounded around the corner and headed upstairs. Jam ran after him, taking the steps two by two. *Poor Boomer. He's chasing Dolley's cat again,* Molly thought, shaking her head with pity.

"How come Boomer's out of prison!" she shouted as her brother ran past her up the stairs.

"Mom said when Pigot leaves, Boomer's home free!" Jam shouted over his shoulder.

Molly saw disaster coming as the huge dog charged up the stairs after the phantom cat. He was running straight for the towering pile of boxes. "STO-O-O-OP!" she shouted with all her might.

But it was too late. Boomer had barreled straight into the boxes, sending them toppling. The gigantic crate teetered on the top step. Molly pressed herself against the wall and held her breath.

In the next second, the heavy wooden crate tumbled down the stairs, hitting each step hard. It landed on the marble entrance floor with a resounding *crash* that sent everyone running to see what happened.

"Pigot's going to go crazy when he sees this," Molly said, running a hand over the cracked crate.

No sooner had she spoken than the decorator came racing down the stairs. "Leave it alone!" he shouted, stumbling in his hurry to stop her.

But it was too late. Molly had already peered inside the crack. And what she saw made her gasp.

Peering back at her were the wise old eyes of President George Washington!

Once the Secret Service agents saw what had happened, they clamped handcuffs on the deflated decorator. "Can't you loosen these cuffs!" Molly heard Monsieur Pigot cry as they hauled him away. "They're pinching my wrists!"

Molly couldn't resist leaving him with a parting remark she had learned from Ama. *Fermez la bouche, Monsieur Pig-o!*" she shouted after him.

"What does that mean?" Jam asked, still puzzled by all the confusion Boomer had caused just by knocking over a pile of boxes.

"I told him to shut his mouth in French," she said with a grin.

Not wanting to be left out, Jam gave Boomer a hug and shouted out the door after them, " 'Justice for all!' " He glanced back over his shoulder at Molly and explained. "D.C.'s state motto."

Molly nodded with a smile. She was sure both Dolley Madison *and* President George Washington would approve.

The following week, Washington's heatwave broke and the White House pools had been filled with water. Molly and Ama didn't waste any time, meeting on Monday morning with their suits already on, by the outdoor pool.

Molly put on her diving mask and looked down at the red, white, and blue flag design on the bottom of the pool. Then she dove in. The water was wonderfully refreshing. She shot up out of the water and climbed onto her air mattress. "You know, Pigot wasn't really such a bad decorator," she said, stretching out on the mattress.

"Just a bad thief," Ama said, lying out by the side of the pool.

Molly looked over at Ama. "Seriously, I wish Mom had let the press in on what happened. We'd be famous. We'd be on the front page of the newspaper."

"We already were!" Jam piped up. "Remember the Potomac River?" He did a cannonball off the diving board, rocking his sister's air mattress.

Molly groaned. "How can I forget? I'm still grounded for two more days. But who cares, now that the pools are filled."

Just then, Mr. Dunbar appeared by the edge of the pool. He hadn't been himself since Monsieur Pigot was sent to prison. "Madam President asked me to remind you—"

At that moment Boomer trotted up to the chief usher and shook his wet fur all over him. Molly covered her mouth to keep from laughing as Mr. Dunbar removed his glasses and carefully wiped them without comment.

"As I was saying," he said, putting his glasses back on, "Madam President asked me to remind you that Boomer is not allowed in the pool."

Jam and the girls burst out laughing as Mr. Dunbar spun around on his heels and hurried across the White House lawn.

Suddenly a pleasant summer breeze blew across the pool, sending tiny ripples across the water. "M-m-m-m." Molly closed her eyes and smelled the lovely floral-scented air.

Just then Molly's hand touched something floating in the water. She scooped it out and lifted it to her face.

A sprig of purple lilac flowers.

White House Fun Facts and Other Cool Stuff

What the White House was like when Dolley Madison lived there:

★ Dolley Madison held the first Inaugural Ball when her husband became president in 1809. That tradition continues today, when there are over twenty balls throughout Washington to celebrate the President's first day in office on January 20.

★ During the Madison Administration, the White House Red Room was the Yellow Drawing Room, where Dolley held her fashionable Wednesday-night receptions. Ever since her famous gatherings, the media have been almost as concerned with life inside the White House as they have been with the president's political views.

★ In 1814, British troops raided Washington. Dolley and the other White House occupants had to leave so quickly that they left their dinner on the table. When the British soldiers came to set fire to the White House, they sat down and finished the dinner at the president's dining-room table first. Only the outside walls and the brick inside walls of the building survived the fire. It took three years to rebuild the White House.

How the Madisons made our country better:

★ James Madison was the main author of the U.S. Constitution. While he was president, he presided over the first major threat to the new nation, the War of 1812.

★ Dolley Madison was used to the duties of the first lady even before her husband was elected President. When her good friend Thomas Jefferson became president, she served as his official White House hostess.

★ Dolley was a natural politician. As first lady, she smoothed over many quarrels between her husband and hostile statesmen. She made all her guests feel at home in the White House, including Native American warrior chiefs and shy children.

Dolley Madison's personality and family life:

★ Dolley Madison was charming and graceful. When Zachary Taylor said that she was truly the "First Lady" of our country, he gave the wife of the president a title still used today.

★ Dolley was self-conscious about being short. She generally greeted her guests dressed in the latest fashions topped by a plumed turban that made her appear taller. Her husband, James Madison, was our shortest president at five feet and four inches.

★ Dolley Madison had a son from her first marriage. Her husband, John Todd, Jr., died in an epidemic of yellow fever when their son Payne was very young. Payne was a very mischievous boy who grew up in the White House with Dolley and her second husband, James Madison.

★ Dolley had a favorite cat, King George, who is a famous White House Ghost, too. He has often been seen curled up in the sun on a window seat or just running around somewhere.

White House improvement? Some presidents made interesting changes to the White House:

★ President Theodore Roosevelt spent much of his time outdoors. He liked hunting so much that he hung a moose head above the State Dining Room fireplace.

★ President Taft was so large he couldn't fit in the bathtub at the White House, so he installed a special tub that was big enough to hold four men.

★ Harry Truman should have restored the White House sooner. During his presidency, a piano leg went right through the floor!

★ President Nixon filled in the White House pool to make more room for the press, but the next president, Gerald Ford, missed swimming. His friends hired workers to dig a new swimming pool on the White House grounds for the president.

Great things you can do to experience a little presidential history:

★ Tour the White House in Washington, D.C., and see the portraits of the presidents and first ladies.

★ Visit Montpelier, the Madisons' home in Virginia, located ninety miles from Washington, D.C.

★ Visit the James Madison Museum in Orange, Virginia, to see some real artifacts from Madison's life.

About the Author

GIBBS DAVIS is the author of several books for young readers. A restless spirit, she divides her time between Wisconsin and New York City.

Although the author has been a fearless ghosthunter for many years, she admits to sleeping with a night-light.